Eyewitness to
Murder

The Hollywood Murder Mysteries

Peter S. Fischer

THE GROVE POINT PRESS
Pacific Grove, California

Also by Peter S. Fischer

THE BLOOD OF TYRANTS

THE TERROR OF TYRANTS

The Hollywood Murder Mysteries

JEZEBEL IN BLUE SATIN

WE DON'T NEED NO STINKING BADGES

LOVE HAS NOTHING TO DO WITH IT

EVERYBODY WANTS AN OSCAR

THE UNKINDNESS OF STRANGERS

NICE GUYS FINISH DEAD

PRAY FOR US SINNERS

HAS ANYBODY HERE SEEN WYCKHAM?

Eyewitness to Murder

ISBN 978-0-9846819-8-3

To my father.....
...who would have preferred I go into business
but gave me his blessing when I turned to writing.
Made it, Pop! Top of the world!

CHAPTER ONE

'm bushed. I don't mean just tired. I mean, wiped out. I flew into L.A. last night from Kansas City after three straight days of chasing one of our newer clients from location to location, from cornfields to small town diners to a city park all dressed up for a Labor Day celebration. The picture is "Picnic" and the stars are Bill Holden and Kim Novak. Our client, Cliff Robertson, plays the hometown guy who loses Novak to Holden. From what I could observe the cast is terrific, the production values are first rate and with a proven property like William Inge's play on which it's based, this film's going to make a lot of money for Columbia Pictures. Harry Cohn may be an unlikeable s.o.b. but he sure knows how to make good pictures.

According to my knowledgeable partner, Bertha Bowles, Robertson is on the brink of stardom. I tend to agree. He is young, handsome, talented and self-assured. He has all the tools. Now we'll see if he has the luck to be in the right movie in the right part. Anybody who tells you that luck has nothing to do with success in Hollywood is either brain-dead or a born loser or maybe both. It's my job to make luck happen. My name is Joe Bernardi and I am one-half of the firm of Bowles & Bernardi, Artists Management.

Until ten months ago I was in charge of press and publicity at

Warner Brothers Studios. Funny, I'd worked there for seven years finally making it to the top job and when I got there, I realized I didn't want it. Maybe I was just tired of battling Jack Warner. Maybe it was the drain of doing the same thing over and over, banging the drum loudly like some 19th Century snake oil salesman often extolling virtues that some of our product didn't actually possess. Maybe at age 34, divorced, and living alone, I wanted to find out if there was more to me than churning out press releases or covering up the peccadillos of pampered wayward stars. That's still part of the package but Bertha's encouraged me to explore other avenues and I'm doing precisely that. In my desk drawer are the first thirty pages of a caper movie involving GI's at the end of WWII. It's short on aesthetics and long on action and if I don't screw it up, I might find myself a career as a screenwriter. I don't know. I'm just groping for a new direction in my life.

Meanwhile I have notebooks full of quotes from Robertson and Columbia's still photographer has promised me several dozen shots of our boy, performing in character as well as hanging around the set with Holden and Novak and the director Josh Logan. My duties are still mainly press and publicity but Bertha is slowly showing me the ins and outs of career planning for our clients which involves a completely different set of muscles.

At the moment I am sitting at my desk going through the mail which accumulated in my absence, all of it carefully laid out by my invaluable right hand gal, the gorgeous Glenda Mae Brown, summa cum laude from Ole Miss, two time homecoming queen and runner up for the title of Miss Mississippi in the Miss America Pageant. She no longer mentions the year in which this miscarriage of justice occurred but she is possessed of magical genes which keep her looking like a college coed no matter what her driver's license says. Glenda Mae tagged along when I handed Jack Warner my resignation and so far, I have seen no sign that she regrets the decision. Thank God. I need her the way Holmes needed Watson.

I am in the midst of scanning a letter from one Antonia Peabody of St. Joseph, Missouri, who claims to be a fifth cousin several times removed to the legendary director, D.W. Griffith. She has written a 320 page screenplay about the Civil War, notable because the ending has the South emerging victorious. She needs my help in finding a producer. She's not going to get it. What she will get is a short polite letter of regret and my best wishes for success elsewhere. Even the rankest of amateurs deserve a kind word and a glimmer of encouragement. Happily letters like this are few and far between.

"Welcome home!"

I look up. Bertha is standing in my open doorway a warm smile on her face. She's a stocky woman who knows how to dress well for her size. She won't divulge her age but I put her at 50 give or take a year. If the stories are true she's had a private life that would make a courtesan blush and though she's never married, over the years she has been linked to two studio heads, three Oscar winners and a United States Senator. No secret, no matter how obscure, is safe from her keen curiosity. If there is something she doesn't know about Hollywood and it's people, she knows where to go to get the answer. Why this legend tapped me to join her as a partner I will never know but so far, it seems to be working out. We have tripled the number of clients we serve, hired seven new employees, and moved into a handsome six room suite on the tenth floor of the Brickhouse Building on Santa Monica Boulevard. I'm making double my Warner Brothers salary and I have a piece of the action. If there is something wrong with this picture, I fail to see it.

I get up from my desk and come around to give her a big hug.

"Glad to be back, Bert," I say.

"How was Kansas?" she asks.

"Flat. Also hot. When are we going to sign Kim Novak?"

"No time soon," Bertha laughs. "She's Harry Cohn's personal property."

"No kidding."

"Only a rumor. I could be wrong. Either way she's got a big future. When the time's right and the bloom is off the Cohn, I'll sit her down for a chat. How'd you like Cliff?"

"Smart. Knows what he wants. I like him."

"It's mutual. We have to find a good followup for him. He needs to firm up his movie credentials. Those dreary live TV dramas served their purpose but he has to move up. Heston and Neilsen did it. No reason Cliff can't."

I nod.

"I hear Columbia's looking for a new leading man for Crawford's next picture," I say.

Bertha frowns.

"You mean the older woman, younger man thing? I thought they had James Dean signed for that."

I shake my head.

"Not according to Josh Logan. He says Dean just signed with Warners to do 'East of Eden' with Kazan."

She sighs.

"Why must it always be Harry Cohn?"

"You want me to take it?" I ask.

She shakes her head.

"I can handle Harry. It's just so damned much work for so little satisfaction." Then she brightens. "So, what's your lunch look like?"

"Nothing,."

"Good. We're meeting with Harold Hecht at Musso & Frank. We may be signing a new client. Swing by my office at 12:45. I'll drive." As she leaves my office, I can't surpress a grin. Harold Hecht is something of a legend in the business. Nine years ago he spotted Burt Lancaster in a short-lived Broadway turkey and recommended him to Hal Wallis for the lead in 'The Killers'. A few years later he and Lancaster formed Hecht-Lancaster and became real players in the producing game. "Apache" and "Vera Cruz", both starring Lancaster, were moneymakers. Whatever the touch is, Harold Hecht has it. This luncheon could turn into something very big.

Musso & Frank is the oldest established Hollywood eatery in town. It's been around since 1919 and you can't name a star or a director or a writer who hasn't eaten there at least once. For most it's been dozens of times and the restaurant's geriatric waiters will tell you in great detail about the time they waited on Pickford or Fairbanks or Orson Welles or the night a fist fight broke out between Hemingway and George Raft. Bert and I walk in at one o'clock sharp. Rico, the maitre'd, swoops in on us like a seagull who has just spotted his lunch in the shallow waters below and armed with menus and leaking more oil than a 1929 flivver, he escorts us to a rear booth where Harold Hecht is already nursing his first martini of the day. Hecht rises, air kisses Bert and shakes my hand with a firm grip. We order drinks and settle in. Small talk first before we order and finally, as Hecht starts on his second martini, we get down to business.

"No offense to you, Bertha, but we really don't need management advice. What we do need is a top notch publicist and there's nobody in town who can match your partner." He raises his glass to me with a smile.

Bertha smiles.

"A lovely compliment, Harold, but we don't take on clients for half the company."

"Of course you don't. This is an all-in deal. We can always use sage advice, especially coming from you, Bertha. But right now we have a picture that just started shooting and we need top of the line press."

"What's the picture?" I ask.

"Marty," he says.

I look at him oddly.

"The TV show?"

Hecht smiles. "Now you know why we need top of the line press."

I share a look with Bertha. I think she's as surprised as I am. I'd heard months ago that someone was considering making a motion picture out of "Marty" but when the talk died down I assumed it was just the latest film deal fallen through. This town is full of them. It's seldom a surprise when a picture doesn't get made. Why? Because you can get fired for green-lighting a turkey but no one ever lost his job for saying 'Don't call us, we'll call you.'

"It's kind of an odd choice for a film," I say.

Hecht knows what I mean. 'Marty' is one of a handful of highly regarded live TV dramas that sprung from New York-based shows like Studio One and Alcoa Playhouse. 'Marty' aired in May of 1953 on the Goodyear Television Playhouse. One of dozens of hour shows known collectively as "kitchen table drama", it was written by a rebellious, wildly talented and fiercely independent playwright named Paddy Chayefsky. Like others in its genre 'Marty' features a minimum of sets, small cast, no action, lots of dialogue and an absence of sex and violence. To make things worse, it has as its two leads a butcher and a school teacher who are middle aged, ordinary and either plain or homely depending on your point of view. A perfect recipe for a hit movie, I think to myself sarcastically.

Hecht is reading my mind.

"Ah, Joe, I know that look. I've seen it a dozen times. Harold, are you out of your mind? Millions of Americans have already seen 'Marty' and they saw it for free so why, in God's name, would they want to pay a buck and a half to see it again in a movie theater?"

"I was thinking the same thing, Harold," Bertha chimes in.

"Well, I'll tell you why, Bertha. Because I think the country is hungry for sentimental drama about real people. I think maybe, just maybe, they'd like a little respite from wide screens and stereophonic sound and pageantry and violence. Chayefsky's done a marvelous job of opening up the teleplay and more fully exploring the characters. I'm convinced and so is Burt that we have a real winner on our hands."

"Well, I do remember that Rod Steiger was awfully good." I hear myself concede.

Hecht shakes his head.

"We don't have Steiger," he says. "We wanted him for a multi-picture contract. He preferred to maintain his freedom so he passed."

"So who did you get?" I ask.

"Ernest Borgnine," he says.

Ernest Borgnine, I think to myself thoughtfully. The guy who played the sadistic Sergeant Fatso in 'From Here to Eternity'. The grinning bully who got the crap beaten out of him by Spencer Tracy in 'Bad Day at Black Rock'. That Ernest Borgnine.

I look at Bertha. She looks back. This project has all the earmarks of a calamity. Even if Borgnine is halfway believable, even if the actress playing the school teacher is effective, even if Chayefsky's revised script is brilliant, what have they got? At best it's a small little black and white art house film that'll do mediocre business for a few weeks and disappear without a trace. It won't be a hit and it certainly won't do enough business to justify the kind of publicity push that I think Hecht is hoping for.

"To be frank, Mr. Hecht, I don't believe I can really help you on this project," I say.

"Call me Harold because I'm going to call you Joe which is the way it should be between two people who are going to be working together now and in the forseeable future." This guy reeks optimism.

"Look, Harold," I say. "You and I both know the pictures that are slated for next year. Picnic. Guys and Dolls with Brando and Sinatra. Oklahoma. Henry Fonda in Mister Roberts. Monroe in

The Seven Year Itch. Hepburn in Summertime. Cary Grant and Grace Kelly in To Catch a Thief. Doris Day in Love Me or Leave Me. Big stars in big pictures. Big canvases. Lots of color. The kind of pictures people can see in a movie theater that they can't see at home on the little 13" box. That's what your "Marty" will be up against and I don't know how to get around that."

Hecht smiles at me.

"You're right, of course, Joe. If this were just another 'little' picture there's every chance we'd get lost in the crowd. But I know something you don't because I've seen the dailies and this is going to be one helluva wonderful film and word of mouth is going to make it a huge success. But for that to happen we have to open and for us to open, we need you."

A picture "opens" when it has a respectable first week's grosses at the box office. If no one knows about it and no goes to see it during that critical first week it'll disappear. Hecht is counting on a big first weekend and neighbor telling neighbor about the picture. Without that the picture is dead.

I sigh.

"As I said—"

"I don't want your answer now, Joe." Hecht says. "Sleep on it. Then fly to New York. Meet with Del Mann, the director, and some of the cast members. Look at the dailies. Then make up your mind. Will you do that much for me?"

I hesitate and look again at Bertha. She is stoic. I can't read her. I do know that we could use a long term relationship with Hecht-Lancaster but how I could possibly publicize this little picture into a must-see event is beyond me. I temporize.

"Okay, Harold, I'll sleep on it. Maybe I'll be struck by some sort of divine inspiration."

"Fair enough," he smiles. "Now who wants a brandy?"

I look again at Bertha. She nods with a slight smile. I've made the right move. Even if I remain unconvinced, which I'm sure I will, I've given Hecht the impression my mind is open. In a day or two I may be able to let him down gently enough to retain his good will.

CHAPTER TWO

efore I head for home, I swing by Jillian's house because I have been invited for dinner. Correction. Actually I invited myself but Jill had no objection and in fact said she'd be glad to see me. I'll be glad to see her. And the baby, of course.

Three years ago Jillian Marx and I were an item. Nothing serious. Good pals. Good bed partners. At least that's the way I looked at it and I had been led to believe she felt the same way, I was wrong. At age 37 she was looking for a husband as well as children and she was all too aware that her biological clock was running down. When it became obvious to her that I was not interested in matrimony and was in fact carrying a torch for someone I hadn't seen or heard from in years, she decided to turn me into a sperm donor. The result was Yvette.

I am a father. It says so on Yvette's birth certificate but that's as far as it goes. With a few exceptions, the rest of the world knows me as kindly Uncle Joe. Yvette will grow up believing this fiction and I will not fight it. It's the pact I made with Jill to forestall any kind of bitter fight over custody and I don't regret the decision. We had a rough time of it early on but we're at peace now. Jill's doing a bang-up job of raising my daughter and I'm content.

I park at curbside and bound up the steps that lead to the front door of Jill's imposing house on Franklin Avenue. Before I can knock she opens the door, baby in her arms and gives me a big smile.

"Look, Yvette, "she says. "Look who's here. Uncle Joe."

Yvette smiles and reaches out a baby fist toward me and says "Unka". That's the best she can do. Even "Unka Joe" is beyond her. I kiss the little fist and then take her in my arms. I give Jill a peck on the cheek as we go inside. A blanket is laid out on the living room floor, littered with Yvette's toys and dolls. I plunk her down in the middle of them and she instantly makes a grab for a nearby rag doll. "Ork" she says holding up the doll and displaying it for me. Yvette speaks a language known only to herself. Jill and I pretend to understand.

At that moment Bridget O'Shaugnessy, housekeeper and governess, appears from the kitchen with a tray on which sits a solitary open bottle of Coors beer.

"I saw you drive up," she says flatly by way of greeting. Sixty-plus, white-haired and opinionated, she sees no reason to fawn over me so she doesn't. I take the beer and thank her with a smile.

"What's for dinner?" I ask.

"Meat loaf," she replies.

"Sounds good," I say.

"It had better," she says as she turns and strides out of the room.

I watch her go and turn to Jill.

"What's the matter with her?" I ask.

"I'm not sure," she says, "but I think Papa Bauer was picked up by the FBI and accused of being a Communist agent."

"What?" I say, totally at sea.

"The Guiding Light," she says, identifying one of CBS's longest running soap operas.

"Ahh," I say with a nod. There are those who live and die with the travails of radio characters. Bridget obviously is one of them.

While the baby plays on her blanket, I tell Jill about my Kansas experience. Like most of the country she's a movie maven and she's delighted to hear that Bill Holden, one of her favorites, is a nice guy. Knowing the play, she has trouble understanding how Holden at age 40 can be playing a drifter in his early 20's. I tell her that moviemaking has a logic all its own. Then I tell her about lunch with Harold Hecht and she looks at me with great skepticism.

"And is that part of Hollywood's logic?" she asks. "Making a movie out of an old TV show people saw for free?"

"An excellent question for which there is no sane answer," I say.

"You are part of a very unreal business, Joe," she says with a disbelieving shake of her head. This coming from a woman who writes children's books about dancing worms, flying zebras, and piano playing spiders.

Over dinner she tells me all about her latest character, a harmonica playing pig named Barnaby who helps a Mama Goat look for her baby kid who has run away from home to visit the Grand Canyon. She says a couple of animators named Hanna and Barbera are looking to break away from MGM and form their own company making kids' cartoons for television. They want Jill to go in with them but Jill's not sure she wants to get involved. Like me she wants to expand her horizons but she's wary of grandiose promises. The movie business has more than it's share of charlatans. I tell her I'll check these guys out and get back to her. I can see she's both grateful and relieved. By eight-thirty the baby's been put in her crib and by eight-thirty-five I'm in my way home to Van Nuys. dog-tired and ready for bed. My little ranch home where I have been living for the past seven years is on a quiet street populated with working class stiffs like my next door neighbor, Chuck Bledsoe, who manages a hardware store. Phil Santini on my other side runs the pro shop at the municipal golf course at Balboa Boulevard. Agatha Pierce behind me is a retired librarian and Eloise Feeney across the street teaches third grade. I'm making enough money now to move to an upscale neighborhood like Brentwood or the Hollywood Hills but why? I like these people, they like me. In a pinch I can call on them for a favor and the reverse is just as true. Besides I like to think they keep me grounded. I'm in a business that reeks of artificiality. Sometimes I lose track of that. The Feeneys and the Bledsoes and the Santinis bring me back to earth.

I park in the driveway and enter the house by the side entrance that opens into the kitchen. My breakfast dishes are still in the sink and the aluminum percolator is half filled with cold coffee. I rinse off the dishes and put them in the rack by the sink. I leave the coffee alone. I'll drink it heated up in the morning. I have a waste not, want not outlook on life born of an impoverished childhood. I'm not proud of it. It just is. I'm about to flip off the light and head for my bedroom when the phone rings. I check the wall clock. Nine-fifteen is an unusual hour for me to get a phone call at home now that I'm no longer working for Jack Warner. I lift the receiver.

"Joe?"

A woman's voice.

"Hi. Who's this?"

"Joe, it's Ginger Tate."

A voice from my past. Six years ago Ginger worked at the Hollywood Reporter as a copy editor, Maybe she still does. At the time she was Bunny's best friend.

"Hi, Ginger, it's been a while," I say.

"I'm sorry to be calling so late. If this a bad time—"

"No, not at all," I say. "What's up?"

There's a strain in her voice. She's badly troubled by something.

"I wasn't sure I should call you. I mean, it really isn't my place but I didn't know what else to do."

"Ginger, what is it?"

After a long pause, she says, "I got a phone call from Bunny."

I can feel my body seize up. I had been trying for years to find

17

Bunny Lesher, my one-time live-in, the one woman for whom I had felt unconditional love. Thousands of dollars, three different private investigators, one dead end after another, chasing a phantom across the country, knowing she was in trouble, desperate to find her, finally giving up the search as a lost cause, resigned to the fact that she didn't want to be found or might even be dead. And now this phone call. Slowly I sit down at the kitchen table.

"When?" I ask.

"Late yesterday afternoon."

"Where is she?"

"New York."

I wince. New York dredges up painful memories.

"She wanted to borrow money, Joe. I think she's in a bad way She sounded awful."

"Is she with someone?" I ask.

"I don't think so. She gave me the name of this shelter. Hang on. I have it here. Just a minute. St. Catherine's shelter for women. I have the address. I think she said it's somewhere on the lower east side of the city." Pause. "Joe, I really am sorry I'm calling you like this—"

"Forget it, Ginger."

"She said she needed three thousand dollars. I haven't got that kind of money."

"I understand."

"Can you help her, Joe?" Ginger asks.

"Sure," I say, "but she may not want me to."

"What are you talking about?"

"She walked out on me, Ginger. Remember that? First to go work at the magazine in New York and then she ran from New York to God knows where. She may not want to see me."

"She will, Joe. I promise you that."

"It's been over five years."

"She loves you, Joe. She always has."

"She told you that?"

"She didn't have to."

"Sorry, Ginger, I'm not buying it."

There's a long silence on the end of the line.

"Ginger?"

"You don't know, do you, Joe? She never told you."

"Told me what?"

Another pause.

"No, it's not my place," she says.

"Told me what, Ginger?" I say more insistently.

"The reason she left you. The reason she ran away."

Now every nerve in my body is tingling. I'd always assumed she'd fallen out of love with me. Or her personal ambition outweighed the possibility of a future together. No, I can see now that it's something else.

"Please, Ginger. I need to hear it," I say.

"You always wanted a big family, didn't you, Joe? You talked about it a lot, she said."

"Sure."

"Bunny couldn't give you a big family, Joe. She couldn't even give you one child. Not even one."

"What are you talking about?"

"That's all I'm going to say, Joe. If you want to know more, ask Bunny. But I'm telling you this. When she left, she loved you as much as she ever did. I don't think that will ever change."

"Ginger—"

"Ask Bunny, Joe. Ask Bunny. Do you want the address of this shelter?"

I tell her I do and she gives it to me along with the name Bunny is currently going by. I write everything down on a pad of paper I keep on the kitchen table.

"What do I say if she calls me again, Joe?"

"Tell her you're working on it. Don't tell her about me. I don't want her running off again."

"Whatever you say."

"Thanks for calling, Ginger."

"Sure. If you see her, tell her we all miss her."

"I'll do that," I say.

After I hang up I stare for the longest time at the address on the writing pad. Then I stand up and dial a number.

"Hello."

"Bert, it's Joe."

"What's wrong?"

"Nothing."

"You sound strange," Bertha saysI

"No, I'm fine," I say. "I've been thinking a lot about our luncheon with Hecht. I've changed my mind. I'm going to New York to check out the picture."

'When?" she asks.

"First thing in the morning."

"You just got back in town. Why don't you take a couple of days?"

"Might as well get it over with. I'll call you from the city."

"You sure?"

"I'm sure."

"Okay. I'll call Harold first thing in the morning and get you the name of the unit manager and his phone number. Where will you be staying?"

"I don't know yet. I'll call you when I'm checked in."

"Okay. Good luck."

"Thanks."

I hang up and grab the yellow pages. I flip to the page headed "Airlines".

CHAPTER THREE

We've just climbed to 12,000 feet and are leveling off. The "No Smoking" sign has been extinguished and the cadaverous guy in the grey suit across the aisle from me can't get those Lucky Strikes out of his shirt pocket fast enough. I'm sitting by a window but I could sit just about anywhere because this flight to New York isn't even half full. Maybe that's because we have two short layovers in Dallas and Nashville and don't get into LaGuardia until nearly midnight. Lesson for the day. Book late and you take what you can get.

I look down as we start to leave San Bernadino behind us. Soon there'll be nothing to see but mountains and desert and only occasional glimpses of civilization. Anyone who thinks we're likely to be strangled by overpopulation has never flown across New Mexico. I reach under my seat and bring up my attache case. I pop it open, eying the bulky manila envelope that contains five thousand dollars in cash as well as my checkbook. I'm ready for anything.

I start to sift through some file folders I have brought with me. The only thing even remotely urgent is a benefit that Bob Hope is staging out in Palm Springs in December for the benefit of the USO. We have two clients he'd like to have volunteer to appear. That's 'volunteer' as in they don't get paid. I think I can deliver. We also have a client that's dying to be invited but so far Hope hasn't shown much interest. A little horse trading may be in the offing.

It isn't long before I lose interest in work and lean back in my seat as thoughts of Bunny creep into my brain. Maybe I'm kidding myself but I remember all the good times vividly even as I try to shove the bad moments into the shadows. I do know this much. I loved her deeply and God help me, I still do. I have not seen her in over four years but when we were together, when we were close, there was a warmth to her that couldn't be extinguished. She radiated optimism and self- confidence and with a smile and a touch of her hand, she could make you feel good about yourself. I know she made me a better person, less self-absorbed, more open to the needs of others.

And then came that magazine convention in New York where she met Walter Davenport who offered her a job at Colliers Magazine. I knew she wanted it. She wanted it badly. She was an insignificant show business reporter on a trade paper that was little known outside of Los Angeles. This was her chance to find out what she was made of and who was I to selfishly tell her no, I want you to stay here with me. I couldn't do it and so I watched her go. Looking back I wonder if part of her decision was to begin separating herself from me. Perhaps so.

We tried bicoastal visits every month but in the end they proved futile and at some point, we found reasons not to travel to the other's bailiwick. Then one day I noticed that her name, always in a minor position, had vanished from the masthead. I called Walt. He told me that regretfully he'd had to let her go. Her work was deteriorating and she was starting to drink heavily. She'd given him no choice. No, he had no idea where she had gone or who she was with. She had literally disappeared.

I hired a private detective to find her. He was useless. I hired another and he was better but he never did catch up with her. His people would get close and then she'd slip away. She started using other names, changing her appearance. Once every few months she'd call. Just to hear my voice, she'd say. She didn't sound well and I was sure she was still drinking. As soon as I started asking if I could help her or where she was located, she'd hang up. After three years and tens of thousands of dollars, I finally gave up looking. If she wanted to see me, she knew where to find me. If not, maybe it was time to face reality. What was, was. It is no longer. Somewhere in the middle of all this ruminating I fall asleep.

We touch down at LaGuardia at ten after midnight. Every bone in my body is stiff and my back is killing me. I won't be moving fast any time soon. By the time I collect my suitcase, hail a cab and make the forty minute trip into midtown Manhattan it's one-thirty when I check into the Astor. My room is waiting for me. It takes me ten minutes to take a hot shower and change for bed. I leave a wake up call and then I crash.

What seems like a minute or two later, the phone rings. I open my eyes. Sunlight is streaming in the windows, half blinding me. I turn away and lift the phone receiver. A woman with a voice like Tallulah Bankhead's tells me it's eight o'clock. I thank her and hang up.

I pad over to my attache case and rummage around for the phone number of the movie company's unit manager. I sit down at the desk and dial it After three rings, he picks up.

"Yeah?" he says brusquely.

I have to assume that Toby Krantz is a busy guy and this morning he sounds especially busy. Unit managers never have good days, only less bad ones. I tell him my name and mention Harold Hecht and almost immediately he puts it together,

"The publicity guy," he says. "Yeah, I heard you might be calling. Mr. Hecht says for me to open all the doors, give you whatever you need."

"Much appreciated," I say. "I thought if it was convenient I'd drop by the set later today and get acquainted."

"Sure," he says. "No problem. Just before lunch we're moving to the Grand Concourse up in the Bronx. My girl'll gjve you directions. Take a cab. It's easier and you won't get lost. Hang on, I'll put her on. Ruby!!!"

A young production assistant comes on the line. Ruby doesn't sound like Tallulah Bankhead, she sounds more like a gangster's moll from the depths of Brooklyn. I write down what she tells me and slip the directions into my wallet, then hang up. My morning is now free which is good because I have somewhere to go. I start to get up from the desk but realize that one thing has been left undone. I need to call Jill.

It's been in the back of my mind since I left L.A. I've tried to shove it aside but I really can't. Bunny was and maybe still is the bugbear in our relationship. The fact that I have flown across the country to be at her side will not sit well with Jill and I constantly live in fear of saying or doing something that will end or limit my access to my daughter. Jill is a reasonable person. If I explain it properly she will understand but at the moment, I have no idea what's going on. No, this is a call I cannot make. Not yet. Not until I have a better grip on the situation.

At ten past nine my cab pulls up to a weather beaten brownstone on Canal Street across from Our Lady of the Sacred Heart church. Like the brownstone, the church shows signs of neglect. It's in bad need of a paint job and the grounds need tending. This neighborhood, on the fringes of Little Italy, teems with tenements and is obviously home to the poorest of the poor, many of them recent immigrants. A few of the local Mamas are already up and about, pushing their baby carriages and chatting on door stoops with their neighbors. There are no youngsters in view because this is the Thursday after Labor Day and the public schools are back in session.

I pay the driver and then hurry across the street where I climb the steps to the front door of the shelter. There is no identifying sign. They have no drop-in traffic. I push the doorbell and hear the chime coming from inside. After a moment the door opens to reveal a burly bald man in a dark suit. He looks me up and down.

"May I help you?" he says.

"Yes. I'd like to see Alice Johnson," I say, giving him the name that Bunny is currenfly going by.

"There's no one here by that name," he says flatly as he starts to close the door.

"Wait!" I say but I'm too late. The door shuts in my face.

I ring the bell again. No response. Again and then again. I try a different approach. I start pounding on the door with my fist. Still nothing. I pound some more and all I get for my efforts is a handful of skinned knuckles. I take off my shoe and start slamming it against the door. Finally I get a response. Once more the door opens.

"If you don't leave I will call the police," the beefy guy says.

"I want to see Sister Veronica Marie," I say to him, "and don't tell me you never heard of her, she signs your paycheck."

"Do you have an appointment?" he asks.

"No," I say, "but I do have a size 12 Florsheim." I hold up my shoe threateningly.

He hesitates for a moment.

"Wait here," he says and once again closes the door in my face. I check my watch. It's 9:26. I'll give the guy four minutes. If he's not back by 9:30 I resume playing Gene Krupa on the front door. I needn't have worried. At 9:30 on the dot he opens the door wide and steps aside. I walk into the foyer which is cramped but also neat and clean and smells of lavender. The big guy moves to a closed door on my right and knocks softly. A woman's voice from inside bids us enter. My host opens the door and again steps back. As I move past him, I can't help but notice the .38 revolver he is carrying in a holster under his left armpit. He notices that I notice. I throw him a feeble smile. He doesn't smile back.

A nun of indeterminate age is sitting behind a desk. I approach. She looks up at me curiously but doesn't invite me to sit. Meanwhile the beefy guy has shut the door and is standing next to it, arms folded across his chest, watching me closely.

"What is your interest in Alice Johnson?" the nun asks.

"I'm a friend."

"Your name?"

"Joseph Bernardi."

She hesitates for a moment.

"May I please see some identification," she says.

I take out my wallet and hand it to her. She scans the contents carefully and then hands it back to me. She gestures to the chair next to me.

"Sit down," she says.

I accept the invitation. She looks over toward the door.

"Thank you, Damien. You may go," she says.

Damien nods and leaves.

"I apologize for what must have seemed rudeness, Mr. Bernardi, but we have a policy about men who come to our door uninvited. Many of the ladies who stay with us while looking for a more permanent situation are battered wives who have run away from abusive husbands. They have found sanctuary here."

I nod. "And if necessary, Damien is on hand to enforce it,"

"Exactly."

"And you are, I presume, Sister Veronica Marie?"

"I am," she says, "and I have been running this shelter for the past six years. I am pleased to meet you, Mr. Bernardi. Alice has spoken of you often."

"Then she's here," I say.

"Yes and no," Sister says. "She has been staying with us for the past eleven days but last night she did not return and I haven't heard from her. At this moment I have no idea where she is."

"Have you checked the hospitals or the police?" I ask.

"The hospitals, not yet. The police? We try to avoid that. Some of our ladies come to us with baggage from prior indiscretions. We prefer to keep all of that within these walls."

"I understand. Do you think she's run off?"

"No. She has fit in here nicely. She'll be back, I'm sure of it."

"Have you any idea where she might have gone?"

"She spends a great deal of time at the nearby meetings of Alcoholics Anonymous. I've called there twice. They haven't seen her either."

"And where would I find this place?" I ask.

She gives me detailed directions and I thank her. I hand her my business card. On the back I've scribbled Hotel Astor and my room number. I ask her to call me if she learns anything. She promises she will. I thank her again and take my leave. Out in the foyer, I find Damien and I thank him, too. It never hurts to cozy up to a guy carrying a gun. He forgets to say 'You're welcome'.

I walk two blocks along Canal, then turn and head toward the Bowery. In the middle of the next block I find what I'm looking for, a deserted storefront whose windows have been painted black on the inside halfway to the top. A faded, barely legible sign over the doorway reads," T. Maggio, Tailor". My guess is that T. Maggio hasn't been around in quite a while. In fact he may be high overhead fitting angels for their celestial gowns. A small white card tacked to the doorframe reads: "Friends of Bill W. 8:00 a.m. 12 noon, 7:00 p.m. Open 24 hours a day. Welcome."

I try the door and it opens. I step inside.

The scene is not unfamiliar. I've been to a few AA meetings in my time, notably when my first wife Lydia was grappling with her disease. There's a lectern set up along the back wall and it faces maybe three dozen folding chairs set up in rows, empty now because the 8:00 is over and the noon is a couple of hours away. Along another wall is the goodie table which holds the cookies and donuts, the hot plate for tea water and a large 30 cup coffee percolator. As I look around a man emerges from the men's room at the back of the storefront. There's always someone on duty around the clock at an AA clubhouse. Demon rum pays no attention to society's concept of time.

"Hi," he says jovially, "I"m Pat." He approaches me with hand outstretched. He's not tall, maybe five-eight and built like a keg of nails. His dark brown hair is military cut and close shaven above the ears. A silver crucifix is strung around his neck and he's wearing an oft-washed Hawaiian shirt not tucked in. I have a sneaky suspicion that under the shirt is a peacemaker nestled into his belt. This is not a great neighborhood and drunks are drunks. Some can get very belligerent.

"Joe," I say, shaking his hand.

"Welcome to the 221 Club. You're late for the eight and a little early for the noon. Want some coffee?"

"No, thanks, " I say. "I'm not here for the meetings. I'm looking for someone."

His eyes narrow slightly.

"Cop?"

"Nope," I say, handing him my card. He checks it out.

"You're a long way from home."

"Flew in late last night. I'm trying to find Alice Johnson."

Pat shrugs.

"Don't think I know her."

"Sister Veronica Marie says she spends a lot of time here. I can waste time by describing her or you can tell me where she is. I know how it works around here, Pat, but believe me, I mean her no harm."

He looks again at my business card.

"Joe," he says. "That Joe? Warner Brothers Joe?"

"I was until late last year," I say.

"She talks about you a lot, Joe," Pat says.

"How's she doing?" "Good, but you know what that means. A thousand days of sobriety and the next day you take a drink. The devil's got you by the throat again."

"I know the drill," I say. "My first wife went through hell until she committed to the program."

"How long?" Pat asks.

"Six years. She's remarried to a great guy, one kid, another on the way."

"Good for her," Pat says.

He walks over to the coffee maker and pours himself a mug of joe. Coffee's the beverage of choice in an AA clubhouse followed closely by orange juice. Tea's a distant third.

"Alice came here sober about two weeks ago from some place in Jersey. She's working on a six month chip. Unless she's slipped, I think she's got a shot."

"Explain that," I say. "Unless she's slipped. What do you mean?"

He loads up up the mug with two creams and three sugars. I've seen milk shakes with less calories.

"I mean I haven't seen her since Tuesday. Normally she'd come to the 8:00 early and then the 7:00 after supper. Yesterday she missed them both."

"You think she's drinking?"

"I don't think anything, Joe. Not yet. Another day or two and yeah, she's drinking. But this, this could be a lot of things."

"Such as?"

"She met a guy, she got a job, she got hurt and is in the hospital, she went home to her folks."

"She hasn't got any folks," I say.

"So she says."

He has put my card on the table. I pick it up and write the name of the Astor on the back along with my room number just as I had done for Sister Veronica Marie. I hand it to him.

"If she shows, will you call me?"

"Possibly," Pat says. "She might not want to see you, Joe."

"I've thought of that," I say. "Three nights ago she called a friend in L.A. and tried to borrow three thousand dollars. She didn't have that kind of money so the friend called me. I have it. If she still needs the money I think she'll see me."

"Okay. I'll tell her we talked, Joe. If she wants to see you, I'll give her the card. Best I can do."

"Good enough," I say, shaking his hand. "And thanks."

I step out the door and take in the sounds and the sights of the street. Traffic is heavy, the sidewalks are crowded, the smells of garlic and onions and peppers pervade the air as the local restaurants prepare for the luncheon crowds which are just minutes away. My spirits are buoyed. Bunny sober six months. I want so desperately to believe it. She has loyal friends in Pat and Sister Veronica Marie. Neither of them is a fool. Maybe at long last my wandering lady is on the road back.

I step into the street and wave as an empty yellow cab heads in my direction.

CHAPTER FOUR

No matter where you are, big city or small town or a country lane in the middle of nowhere, you can always find a movie company on location. Just look for a half dozen bigrig trailers, a few smaller units towed by pickup trucks, three or four motor homes, a gaggle of people either hustling quickly in every direction carrying flood lamps and boom mikes or more often than not, sitting around smoking and jawing with one another. At the periphery of this activity, depending on the population density of the locale, will be a gathering of onlookers as well as a security force to keep them from disrupting the filming.

As soon as we turn onto the Grand Concourse, I spot the company and I direct my driver to pull to the curb as close as he can to the action. I pay him and hop out. I have no enthusiasm about being here. I still believe this film is financially a lost cause but I promised I'd look into it and so that's what I'm doing. I fully anticipate calling Bertha tonight to tell her that this isn't for us.

I've taken no more than a dozen steps forward when a uniformed cop blocks my way, I check his shoulder patch. This is no rent-a-cop, this guy is NYPD. Hecht must really be well connected to get the city to pony up a security force for this relatively minor motion picture.

I hand the guy my business card and tell him I'm supposed to be meeting Toby Krantz, the unit manager, whom I haven't yet met. The cop nods, jabbing a finger toward a man who is standing beside the caterer's lunch wagon, deep in conversation with a young woman holding a clipboard. I head over to him. Krantz is a tall ungainly guy with a pot belly shaped like a basketball. His hair stands up on his head almost like a fright wig and he seems to be staring at the world disapprovingly through wire-rimmed Granny-glasses.

"Mr. Krantz?" He looks at me like I might be a bill collector. "Joe Bernardi," I say. "We talked on the phone." An expression crosses his face that some people might mistake for a smile.

"Oh, yeah," he says. "Nice to meet you." He puts out his hand and we shake but he's clearly a man with troubles.

"If this is a bad time," I start to say.

"No, no. We just cracked a lens and the backup's no good so we had to send out for a new one. Gonna cost us a couple of hours, at least."

One of the pitfalls of movie making, dealing with the unexpected. The bottom line is always time and money and when you're operating on nickels and dimes the way this company is, the simplest problem is a crisis.

"Are you okay on your permit?" I ask.

"It's good until midnight but when we run out of daylight, we're through. Mann's gonna print a lot of first takes."

Delbert Mann's the director. As I recall he also directed the television version. In fact, I think this may be his first motion picture. "How's he doing?"

Now Krantz does smile.

"He knows his stuff. So, you hungry, Mr. Bernardi? How about lunch?"

"Sure, and how about calling me Joe?"

"Joe, it is," he says. "And I'm Toby." Then "Ruby!!!" he bellows. From out of nowhere appears a wraith in khakis and a blue windbreaker, long brown hair flying in every direction around her head.

"Here, boss," she says breathlessly in vintage Brooklynese.

"Fix Mr. Bernardi a tray. We're going over and say hi to Ernie."

"Right, boss," Ruby says and then looks at me. "You want fish, chicken or mystery meat?" she asks.

"Ooh, that doesn't sound good, " I say.

"Bet your life on that," she replies.

I smile at her.

"Surprise me," I say.

"Your funeral," she shrugs and hurries away.

Toby leads me to the eating area where a couple of dozen crew members are chowing down, chatting or smoking. Two trestle tables and about forty folding chairs have been set up some twenty feet from the lunchwagon where the caterer prepares the midday menu. Borgnine is sitting at the end of one of the tables, talking to a couple of grey-haired guys who I take to be crew. He looks up as we approach.

"Ernie, say hello to Joe Bernardi. He's going to be handling publicity on the picture," Toby says.

Borgnine gets to his feet and extends his hand with a broad smile. "Nice to meet you, Joe. Say hello to Sid and Benny."

Hellos and handshakes all around as I learn that Sid is the gaffer and Benny is the propmaster. Borgnine clears a space next to his.

"Sit down, Joe. You want some lunch?"

"Ruby's getting me a tray," I tell him.

"Oooh, Ruby," Sid says as in ooh-la-la, making lascivious hand gestures in the process.

"Knock it off, Sid," Ernie says. "She's a nice kid and she's only twenty. Pick on somebody your own age."

"Need an old folks home for that," Benny says straight-faced.

"Screw you guys," Sid says, taking a bite of his buttered roll.

Ruby appears with my tray and sets it down in front of me. Fried chicken, mashed potatoes and broccoli and a paper cup filled with chocolate pudding.

"Thanks, Ruby. Looks good," I say.

She shrugs.

"The least disgusting things on the menu. You won't throw up," she says and stomps off with the gait of a bouncer looking for a fight to pick. She may only be twenty but I make a note not to get in her way.

We spend a couple of minutes gabbing about the pennant race which is the talk of the town. The Giants are in first but the Dodgers are only a handful of games behind. Borgnine says the Giants have it sewed up and will beat the stuffing out of the Indians in the Series. Benny thinks the Dodgers can still pull it out. Sid says the Dodgers are chokers ever since 1951 and the Bobby Thompson homerun. He says the Dodgers are dead for at least a decade, maybe longer. so maybe they should get out of Brooklyn while the getting is good. I keep my mouth shut because my team, the Cardinals, is pathetically trapped in the second division, a bunch of hapless losers.

Benny and Sid leave to go back to work and Borgnine and I have a chance to chat. The more we talk, the more I like this guy. He's no more like sadistic Sergeant Fatso than Fred Astaire is like Wallace Beery. We trade war stories. While I was writing about the dogfaced infantrymen in Europe, he was fighting the Japs in the Pacific. Interestingly he'd joined the Navy in '35 when he graduated high school but then mustered out in '41. When the Japanese hit Pearl Harbor he re-upped immediately and spent the war aboard a destroyer as a Chief Gunners Mate. In '45 with a chest full of medals he came home to Hamden, Connecticut. The war finally over, he'd had enough of the Navy.

"There's nothing glamorous about war," Ernie says. "You know. You were there. Folks who stayed home, they had no idea. None at all." He sips at his coffee. "My Mom, she's the greatest. I get home. Big hero, that's me. Everybody's patting me on the back. Mom's feeding me breakfast every morning. Whatever I want. I'm loafing around the house because, like I said, I'd had enough of the Navy but I don't know what I want to do with myself. Then after about three weeks, I'm laying in the hammock in the backyard and Mom comes out to hang up the wash and she looks at me with this expression in her face and she says, 'Well?' And I know what she means. It's time I got myself a job." He laughs and shakes his head. "Moms are great," he says. "They always have it right." I don't tell him I wouldn't know because I never had one. We chat like that for a few more minutes and then he gets called for makeup. The camera must be fixed. He heads off for the makeup trailer and I go looking for Toby Krantz. I find him talking to the driver captain going over the next day's shoot at White Plains Road. When they finish Toby walks me to the street. He apologizes for not giving me a lift back to the Astor but he hasn't got a driver or a vehicle he can spare.

"We look at dailies at six o'clock," he says. "You're welcome any time." He takes out a card and scribbles on the back, then hands it to me. "This hotel is headquarters for the next two and a half weeks. The number on the back is a direct line to the production office on the lower level. If I'm not there, talk to Ruby or Greg."

"Thanks," I say, taking the card. "Out of curiosity, just what is the budget?"

"Three-fifty," Toby says.

I'm not shocked. I expected a low number but not that low. It's tough making a quality film for three hundred and fifty thousand dollars but as I look around I get the feeling that this bunch might just pull it off.

"Tight squeeze," I say.

"We'll manage," Toby says. "So what do you think of Ernie? Not quite what you expected, right?"

"No, he isn't," I admit.

"This movie's full of surprises, Joe. Has been from the beginning. Don't sell us short. A lot of people think we're wasting out time making a hotsy-totsy art house movie here but they're wrong. Something special is going on with this picture, trust me."

I nod. I'm beginning to think he's right.

"I'll try to make this evening's dailies," I say.

"See you then," Toby says as I spot a cruising cab and wave him to the curb.

We head down Broadway, then scoot over to the West Side Drive. From there it's a straight shot to the midtown Manhattan exit ramp. We start across town which is when we get stuck at a light next to a city bus. I look over and find myself staring at the face of an old friend who is the subject of a huge billboard ad that stretches from the driver's window to the tailpipe. John Crosby covers television for the New York Herald Tribune and most people agree, he's number one in his field. A sharp and perceptive critic, he writes with an engaging style and has no illusions about the scope of his influence. First comes the theater critic, then the movie critic and then John. In an era of reviewing live television dramas, sometimes more than one an evening, he once referred to himself as a man whose sole job it was to describe a ten car auto accident to millions of eyewitnesses.

I've known him for the past ten years, ever since we met in France, a couple of months after D-Day. I was writing for 'Stars and Stripes' and John was a Captain in Army News Services. When Paris was abandoned by the Krauts in late August I found myself in a unit headed by John cranking out stories for the home front about the brave exploits of the city's liberators, Most of what we wrote about the G.I.'s and the Brits was true. When it came to lauding the French, we held our noses. After about ten days John was shipped back to London and I headed south to hook up with Patton's 3rd Army.

Jump forward to '51. I'm here in the city for one of my Bunny visits when I run into John in the lobby of the Waldorf-Astoria. Bunny's tied up at the Colliers office until supper and John's at loose ends after lunching with Edward R. Murrow for a column about Murrow's new CBS show, "See It Now". We retire to the bar for the next two hours where we get well-lubricated dwelling on old times. Neither of us wants to relive them. Ever. We agree that Korea is a senseless tragedy. We drink to a quick end to the war. We drink to Harry Truman for standing up to that insufferable egomaniac, Douglas MacArthur. We drink to Eisenhower who may be our next President and who will bring the boys back home. By the time we are ready to leave, we are reduced to drinking to the Duke of Windsor, don't ask me why.

As the cab pulls up to the Astor's main entrance I make a mental note to call John for dinner or drinks or maybe both. Not only would I like to renew an old acquaintance, I'd like to get his opinion on this movie remake of "Marty" which, as I recall, was one of his favorite all-time television dramas.

The little red light on my bedside telephone is blinking. I call down to the desk and am told I have a message. Sister Veronica Marie called at 12:15. I jot down the number she left and as soon as I'm finished with the message desk, I call the shelter.

"What news, Sister?" I ask when she comes on the line.

"A police sergeant showed up shortly after you left this morning, Mr. Bernardi." she says. "He was asking a lot of questions about Alice."

"Is she in trouble? Is she hurt?"

"No, she's in jail. She was picked up off the streets two nights ago."

"On what charge?" I ask, simultaneously feeling anger as well as fear.

"Solicitation," she says.

"That's baloney," I say. With a nun, i use words like 'baloney'.

"He asked a lot of questions. I got the feeling Alice was in serious trouble."

Sister gives me the cop's name and tells me he works out of the 9th Precinct. I thank her and promise to be in touch as soon as I learn something.

CHAPTER FIVE

My cab pulls up to 130 Avenue C, home of New York's Ninth Precinct in lower Manhattan. I tell the cabbie not to wait even though this is a pretty grungy neighborhood where I suspect cabs cruise infrequently. I climb the stairs and step into the gloom of the main floor which at this hour of the day is pretty deserted. I wouldn't want to be here on a Saturday night, not without a bodyguard. I walk over to the desk sergeant and tell him I'm looking for Sergeant Horvack whose name was on the card given to Sister Veronica Marie. The desk sergeant points to a staircase. Second floor, turn left, he tells me.

The squad room is busy. Several cops are taking statements from either witnesses or miscreants, I can't tell which. Two others are on the phone. Another is hunting and pecking away at his typewriter filling in a report. I have yet to meet a cop who has even a nodding acquaintance with touch typing. Maybe skill with two fingers is a job requirement for NYPD detectives. I see a cop in shirt sleeves at a nearby desk poring over a file folder and decide to use him as an information center.

"Excuse me, maybe you can help me. I'm looking for Sergeant Horvath,"

He raises his head from his work.

"You're looking at him," he says. Detective Sergeant Karol Horvath is a slim blonde athletically built man most likely in is early 30's with wide set blue-grey eyes and high Slavic cheekbones. His hair is cut longish and neatly combed, swept back over his ears and his expression is one of wary curiosity.

"My name is Joseph Bernardi. I'm a good friend of Alice Johnson and I'd like to see her."

"Sorry. Not possible," he says. "Only spouses, blood relatives and attorneys permitted."

"I'm her husband," I lie.

His face breaks into a grin.

"Nice try, sport, you blew that when you said you were a good friend."

"Look, Sarge, I'm not a lawyer but—"

"We can all be grateful for that," Horvath interrupts.

"—but solicitation is a pretty low level beef. Why the freeze out?"

"You'd have to ask her lawyer."

"And what's his name?" I ask.

"She hasn't got one," Horvath says with a wry smile.

Oh, great, I think. A clown for a cop. And then Horvath's expression turns more serious.

"Look, Mr. Bernardi. We have one count of solicitation, one count of resisting arrest, one count of battery on the person of a police officer and one count of fleeing the scene of a crime. The fact that she doesn't want a lawyer is her business, not yours and not mine, and now if you'll excuse me I'm busy." He turns his attention back to his file folder.

I watch him for a moment and then I say, "I'm going out to make a phone call, Sergeant, and then I will return. I'll be downstairs waiting on one of the benches when you need to find me."

"And why the hell would I want to do that?" Horvath asks.

I just smile.

"Downstairs. Bench," I say with a smile and then I turn and walk out of the room.

I walk across the street to a bank and trade in a ten dollar bill for a pocketful of quarters, dimes and nickels. I go in search of a phone booth and find one in the pool parlor at the end of the block. After I've fed the phone enough coins to feed a family of four for a week, I get connected to the office.

"Bowles and Bernardi," comes the throaty come-hither voice. Greta, our gorgeous receptionist, boasts a Marlene Dietrich timber without the accent. Clients call us just to hear her speak and maybe if they're lucky, hustle her into a dinner date. They don't succeed because I have it on good authority (Glenda Mae) that Greta has her eye on me. I'm flattered but not interested but I try not to discourage her. Really good receptionists are hard to find.

"Hi, Greta, it's me," I say.

"It is so nice to hear your voice, Mr, Bernardi. How is New York?"

"Smug," I say. "Is Mrs. Bowles in?"

"She has someone with her. Mr. Preminger, I think."

"Buzz through. Tell her it's urgent and I'm running out of quarters."

"Just a moment," Greta says, putting me on hold. Within the next minute, Bertha comes on the line.

"Your timing's lousy. Otto was just about to invite me out on his yacht for the weekend."

"Otto doesn't have a yacht. It's a rowboat."

"Don't get bitchy just because you have no personal life. What's up with the picture?"

"I'll call you about that tonight. Meanwhile I need a favor. Didn't you once tell me you knew Mayor Wagner?"

"Bob? Sure, " she says. "I was hustling for investors for two or three big Broadway producers and he was this kid lawyer right out of Yale looking to get himself connected."

"How well did you know him, Bert?"

"Let's not get too personal here, partner."

"Well enough to call him in the next ten minutes and ask a favor?"

Her tone becomes suspicious.

"What kind of favor?" she asks.

I give her a five minute explanation and for a few moments there is silence coming from her end.

"Is that why you flew to New York, Joe? Because of her?"

"Partly. Again we'll talk tonight. Meanwhile, yes or no? I need this, Bert."

Bertha knows all about my past with Bunny. She's sympathetic to a point but she thinks I've let this quest consume me. She may be right but at the moment I'm not in the mood to argue it.

"Hecht-Lancaster could be a big catch, Joe. I don't want to lose them."

"We won't," I say.

"We will if they think we're jerking them around on this picture. You're either in New York for the company or you're not, Joe. Which is it?"

"I'm going to do my job, Bert," I tell her.

"Open mind?"

"Absolutely."

"The picture comes first, Joe. The lady's in second position."

"All right."

"I mean it, Joe."

"I said all right, Bert," I say testily.

"I'll see what I can do," she says finally.

I tell her that's good enough for me and I hang up. I'm a little annoyed but I realize she's right. Burt Lancaster is an A List star and this little independent company could turn into a giant. I owe them a fair shake and I owe Bertha honesty. I should have told her what I was up to from the start. Partners don't keep secrets. I won't make this mistake again. I hurry back to the police station and take up a spot at the end of one of the benches. I check my watch. The time is 3:10. The wait begins.

At 4:25 I look up and see Horvath coming down the staircase. About half way down our eyes meet,. He points a finger in my direction and then waves me upstairs. The wait is over.

"I don't know who the hell you know, buddy," he says, locking up his desk, "but my Captain says if you suggest carnal relations, I'm to bend over without protest."

"Unlikely it will come to that," I say with a smile.

"My wife will be pleased to hear it." He slips on his suit jacket. "Who's your godfather?"

"Sorry. Can't say."

He glowers at me for a moment, then shakes his head.

"Let's go," he says.

We go downstairs and out a rear door where an unmarked car is waiting for us. Horvath slips behind the wheel while I climb in the passenger seat. We pull out into the street and head across town.

"Where are we going?" I ask.

"Manhattan Criminal Court Building," he says. "That's where we have her stashed."

That's an odd phrase. I look over at him.

"Stashed? What do you mean, stashed?"

"We've dropped the charges. She's being held as a material witness."

"Witness to what?" I ask.

"Murder," he says.

As he drives, Horvath fills me in. Bunny, or Alice Johnson as she is known to the police, was picked up on a street corner in the company of a known prostitute named Daphne Gennaro. Horvath admits it was a dumb bust. A couple of young officers in a squad car being overzealous. The older guys wouldn't have given them a second look. Even then it should have been nothing but the one called Alice got pissed off and slugged one of the cops with her purse and then tried to run away. So they brought them to the precinct a little before nine-thirty and locked them up in one of the cells in the back of the station house. This after Daphne makes her one phone call, apparently to her boyfriend, who incidentally does not show up. Then around three in the morning the guys out front hear screaming coming from the back. Two of them hustle into the holding area and there's one of the babes backed up against the wall screaming her lungs out and the other one lying in a pool of blood on the floor, half her head blown away. When they finally get things quieted down, the screamer—your friend Alice—says that a guy dressed as a cop approached the cell, took out a large pistol with a silencer attached and fired point blank at her friend's head. She never knew what hit her. Then he turned his gun on Alice who was still screaming. For whatever reason, the gun jammed and when the guy heard approaching voices, he turned and ran out the back.

I shake my head in disbelief.

"Jesus," I mutter quietly.

"Yeah," Horvath says. "Could have been a real cop though I doubt it. More likely a guy who stole or rented a uniform."

"How'd he get in?"

"There's a rear door for deliveries. It's always locked, but if this guy was a pro, which we think he was, a lock wasn't going to stop him."

I nod in agreement.

"I assume you're looking at the other girl's boyfriend. I mean, who else knew she was locked up in your holding area?" I say.

Horvath nods.

"The phone company gave us the number she called. The phone's listed to a Harvey Claymore Jr. at his flat in Greenwich Village. The call was placed at 9:35 and the duration of the call was two minutes and twenty five seconds."

"And?"

"We ran down Mr. Claymore Jr. today and he denied he received the call. He said he was at his father's apartment on the upper East Side for dinner, stayed for a bridge game and spent the night in a guest bedroom."

"Do his parents back him up?"

"Father. His mother Lila died in a traffic accident three weeks ago. An ugly hit and run. The papers were full of it. Anyway, the old man backs him up. So does the couple they were playing bridge with."

"Yet somebody answered that phone in Greenwich Village," I say. "So says the phone company," Horvath says as he turns into the parking lot that services the Manhattan Criminal Court Building.

I frown. This isn't making a lot of sense.

"The shooter. Was he masked?" I ask.

"No," Horvath says, "and before you ask, Claymore Jr. looks nothing like your girlfriend's description."

And on that note, we exit the car and start inside the mammoth building. Located at 100 Centre Street, it boasts four huge towers that rise seventeen stories above the street and is home to both the Criminal and the Supreme Courts, the offices of the District Attorney as well as various arms of the New York Police Department, including Corrections. Horvath and I pass through two separate security checkpoints before we arrive at the holding area.

"Think she'll be safe here?" he asks a little smugly.

"As long as all the cops are real," I say.

He stops smiling.

"I'll arrange for an interrogation room," Horvath says.

"No," I say. "I'll talk to her in her cell."

Horvath shakes his head.

"I can't let you do that."

"Look," I tell him, "the lady and I may have some very personal things to say to one another. I would prefer you and a bunch of voyeurs not be peering at us through a one-way window."

"Well, that's the way it's going to be, Bernardi. Take it or leave it."

"I hear foot patrol is a bitch these days in Harlem."

"Don't bullshit me, Bernardi, I'm not in the mood."

"Up to you," I say. "Lead me to a phone."

He hesitates.

"Just who is your juice, pal?"

"You remember in Flash Gordon, Ming The Merciless, he who answers to no one. Well, my juice answers to no one but the voters."

Horvath stares at me for one disbelieving moment before he realizes I'm not kidding.

"I'll see about that cell," he says and walks off.

A few minutes later a guard jangling a large set of keys is leading me into the holding area. I look to my left to a small single cell and I see her curled up in a fetal position in her cot, her back toward me. The guard unlocks the door and lets me in and then re-locks the door. We've arranged that he will be close by but not close enough to hear what we are talking about.

I approach the cot.

"Bunny?"

I see her body tense and then freeze. After a long pause, she turns and looks up at me. Her eyes are wide and I don't know if it's surprise or disbelief or maybe even shame. It may be a combination of all three.

CHAPTER SIX

"Joe?" she says haltingly. "What are you doing here?"

"Answering a cry for help," I say.

She sits up but makes no effort to stand. She's been looking into my eyes. Now she looks away. She looks terrible and I think she knows it. She's at least twenty pounds lighter than when last I saw her. Her hair is cut short and shaggy and while it appears newly washed, the color is a musty brown. Her skin, always clear and robust looking, is sallow. She is wearing little or no makeup.

"I don't want you seeing me like this. Please go."

"Too late now," I say. "Everyone's worried about you."

"Tell them I'm fine," she says.

I ease myself down on the end of the cot.

"You're not fine. What happened, Bunny?"

She shakes her head, still not looking at me.

"Look, I'm here to help and I'm not leaving until you let me. If they pull me out of this cell, I'll be waiting for you downstairs. If they toss me from the building I'll be waiting on the sidewalk. Like it or not, I am here for you. I came because you tried to borrow three thousand dollars from Ginger. She called me because she didn't have it but she knew I did. Now I've brought the money and why you need it is something we can discuss later. Meanwhile, I want to know what happened. How did you end up here in this situation?"

She shakes her head.

"Joe, I know you mean well—"

"Bunny, you're not listening. I'm here. I'm involved. I'm not going anywhere. Now, please. Tell me. Who was this Daphne person? How did you get mixed up with her?"

"It's complicated."

"I've got all day and all night."

She stares off into space and for a long time she says nothing. Finally she looks at me.

"I met her about a week ago at a meeting."

"I know about the 221 Club. Pat's worried about you."

She manages a faint smile.

"He would be. Mother hen."

"Maybe so, but you've got a friend there. Now, about Daphne."

"She was new. I was new. We gravitated toward each other. She told me her story. I told her mine. She was a nice kid."

"Kid?"

"Twenty-five. By me that's a kid. She came to New York five years ago looking to make it as a singer.She got mixed up with agents and club owners and a lot of other unsavory characters. It just didn't happen for her which is how she got hooked up with Alma Willows."

"Don't know her."

"She runs a high class escort service for discriminating gentlemen, that's how Alma describes her business. I'd heard of her when I worked for Walt at Collliers. I didn't need a road map."

"Not a fun way to make a living," I say.

"I wouldn't know, Joe. I sank pretty low but never that low."

I nod. "About a year ago she met Junior. Harvey Claymore Junior. Thirty something with the mindset of a teenager. A good looking good time Charlie from a rich family. He rescued her from the business and set her up in an apartment on Park Avenue. After a while he started talking marriage. Daphne didn't really love the guy but thought maybe it was a good idea. She knew what kind of options she had and they were all lousy. Junior works for his father, Harvey Claymore Sr., in real estate and he had neglected to tell his old man about Daphne because he was pretty sure his father wouldn't be happy about her and especially about the idea of marriage."

"Where's his mother in all this?" I ask.

"Dead. She was hit by a truck in broad daylight crossing a street a few weeks earlier. The truck fled the scene. His mother died in the ambulance on the way to the hospital. The old man was devastated. Couldn't sleep, couldn't eat. Junior knew there was no way he could tell his father about Daphne. Not at that moment. And then Junior made the mistake of confiding in his younger brother Biff who is a flake and a rebel and who is all caught up in some kind of auto racing and wants nothing to do with the family business. Junior admires Biff's free spirit but Daphne had the idea that Biff hated his brother because of the way Junior was always sucking up to the old man. Anyway, however it happened, Biff told Senior about Daphne."

"And all hell broke loose," I say.

Bunny nods.

"The father went crazy, threatened to disown Junior if he saw or talked to Daphne ever again. He pressured someone in the housing department to squeeze her landlord and in less than 24 hours, Daphne was out on the street, evicted from her apartment. Junior was scared to death. He's kind of a gutless guy and he didn't know what to do which is when Daphne tells him she's pregnant. Junior thought maybe the news of a baby would make his father relent but it made the old man even more furious. His son having a baby by some two bit whore. The old man told Junior to take care of the problem any way he had to and to do it right away or he could get the hell out of the house, the business and the family."

"When was this?" I ask.

"Three days ago," Bunny says.

I shake my head in disbelief.

"Jesus," I mutter under my breath.

"He had her killed, Joe. I know he did."

"Junior?"

"Yes, Junior. He didn't have the guts to do it himself. He hired somebody but he did it, Joe. He as good as pulled the trigger himself."

"And the man who sneaked into the police station, are you sure it wasn't Junior?"

Bunny shakes her head.

"No, I met him once when he came by a meeting to see her."

"And how was it you got yourself arrested?"

She shakes her head. Her eyes are misting and she's on the verge of tears.

"Do we have to talk about this?"

"Yes, we do. Bunny," I say sharply, trying to shake her into reality. "Do you realize how much danger you're in? You're an eyewitness to a murder. You're lucky you aren't already dead. Whoever killed your friend knows he's in trouble as long as you're alive to identify him and if he gets the chance to finish the job, he's going to take it."

She looks up at me wide-eyed. It was tough to hear and tougher for me to say but she can't be allowed to roll up into a ball of denial.

"I'm sorry I had to put it so bluntly but you have got to face your situation. Now I need to hear your story, Bunny. All of it."

After a moment, she nods slowly. "Daphne missed a couple of meetings and I got worried so I went looking for her. There's this greasy spoon a few blocks away where we'd stop for coffee and a danish so that's where I looked. She wasn't there but I hung around in case she showed. Sure enough she came by around six thirty. We sat and talked for a long time and then around nine o'clock we went outside. We were standing around on this street corner, still talking and chasing away a few wiseguys who took us for working girls when this squad car pulled up. These two punk cops started giving us a hard time because the local cops all knew who Daphne was and where she came from. Anyway I gave it right back to them. One of them grabbed me and I slugged him with my purse and tried to run for it which was when the heel on my shoe broke off and I'm not running anywhere. Next thing I know me and Daphne were being shoved in a jail cell at the back of the 9th Precinct."

"Before or after she makes a phone call to Junior to come and get her out?" I ask.

"Before," she says. "And that's why I think Junior had her killed, Joe, because nobody else knew that she was being held by the cops in that station house."

I have to admit that makes sense but even so, Daphne's murder is brazen and risky. It's either the act of someone incredibly stupid or the reverse, someone with balls of brass who knew exactly what he was doing.

"Tell me about the shooter," I say.

"I didn't even see him until the last second. I was kind of dozing and I opened my eyes and he was standing there with this gun in his hand and he was pointing it at Daphne. Before I could say anything or scream he pulled the trigger and it made this dull quiet sound and I looked over and Daphne'd slammed back against the wall and where her face used to be all I could see was blood. Then the guy swung the gun around and pointed it at me and I started to scream. That's when he tried to pull the trigger again but nothing happened. I screamed a lot louder as he tried to pull the slide back but it wouldn't move and then I heard voices coming from the front of the station and the guy turned and ran toward the back.

A couple of seconds later two cops ran into the holding area. I'm still screaming and I point to the rear and one of them goes chasing after the shooter but it's too late. He got away."

"The sergeant says you got a good look at him."

She nods.

"Sort of tall, black hair, sideburns down to his jaw line like a greaser. Thick black eyebrows and cold eyes, Joe. Icy cold. He didn't try to hide his face."

"That's because he didn't intend to leave behind any witnesses. Have you looked at any mug books?"

"Some. I didn't see his picture."

I say. "Look, Bunny, I think you're safe in here for the time being but I'm not sure how long they can hold you like this. I'm going to get a lawyer and see if I can get you released."

She nods her head without saying anything. I reach over and take her hand,. She doesn't try to draw it away. She looks up at me.

"Why are you doing this, Joe?" she asks.

"You know why, Bunny," I say.

"No, not after all this time. The way I've treated you. I can't let you do this, Joe. It isn't fair."

"Let me worry about fair. I love you, Bunny. Always have and always will and if this doesn't go any further than helping you get out of this mess you're in and getting you back on your feet, well, that'll be okay. This is all about you, not me. Now let me help."

"All right," she says quietly and I feel her squeeze my hand tightly.

I get up and walk over to the cell door. I signal to the guard who is sitting on a folding chair at the end of the corridor. I turn back to Bunny.

"Out of curiosity, the three thousand dollars,. What was that all about?"

"It doesn't matter now," she says,

"Humor me."

"There's this hospital in White Plains. Smith-Lerner. They have a sixty day rehabilitation program for alcoholics. I thought maybe they could help me put my life back together."

I nod.

"Maybe they can." The guard opens the cell door wide for me. "Rest up now. I'll be in touch with you later."

I go out. As I head for the elevator, I check my watch. It's six-fifteen. I've missed the 'Marty' dailies. Okay, so I'll go tomorrow evening. Meanwhile I go in search of Sergeant Horvath.

I find him sitting alone at a table in the lower level cafeteria. He's dabbing at something that contains a variety of cutup food stuffs mostly disguised by thick brown gravy.

"What is that?" I ask, pointing to his plate.

"Dinner," he says. "I couldn't stand the thought of going home to my wife's pot roast, mashed potatoes, corn on the cob and a peach cobbler for dessert so I decided to settle for Typhoid Manny's beef stew since I had to be here anyway baby sitting this out of town pain in the ass who may or may not be the Mayor's fifth cousin from Los Angeles."

I stare down at him.

"I'm going to get myself a coffee," I say.

"I take mine black, no sugar," he says.

I nod my head and head for the bank of percolators. I return in less than a minute and slide the mug of joe toward him.

"Sorry if I screwed up your evening," I say.

"Forget it. Happens all the time. New York, the town that never sleeps. Neither do its cops." He sips a little coffee. Still too hot to drink. He takes a rumpled pack of cigarettes from his shirt pocket and lights up, inhaling deeply and blowing the smoke out of his nose.

"How long do you plan on holding her?" I ask.

"As long as I have to," he says.

"That's not true."

"You a lawyer?"

"No," I say, " but the guy I hire will be. I want her out of here."

"She's safe with us," Horvath says.

"Like she was safe at the Ninth Precinct?"

"If she leaves here she's an easy target. This shooter, he'll be looking for her."

"He won't find her."

"Says you, Mr. Bernardi." He leans back in his chair and regards me with an expression that borders on amusement. "You really don't know who you're messing with, do you?" he says.

"Suppose you tell me," I say.

"Harvey Claymore Senior, president and chief stockholder of Claymore Properties, a privately held corporation with assets that reach into the tens of millions. Maybe more. Confidant of politicians and powerful union leaders, socially connected to local businessmen named Gambino and Anastasia and other kinsmen of yours, Mr. Bernardi, he's probably worth ten or twelve million dollars. When he sneezes, city councilman wipe his nose for him. He has two sons, neither one of which is worth the spare change he keeps in his pocket to hand out to street bums. Anything else you'd like to know?"

"Is he capable of hiring someone to walk into a police station dressed as a cop and commit a cold blooded murder?"

"Does Cardinal Spellman eat fish on Friday nights?"

"Like that."

"Yes, Mr. Bernardi, like that."

"And if his son was the one who did the hiring—?"

"No difference. No matter how much contempt he might have for the two of them, they're all he has left. "

"So when you investigate this shooting—IF you investigate this shooting—"

Horvath glares at me.

"I'll do my job, Mr Bernardi," he says. "I'll do it carefully but I'll do it."

"I'm relieved to hear it," I say icily. "I'll see you tomorrow, Sergeant. With my lawyer."

"Good luck," Horvath says, extinguishing his cigarette in the middle of his plate of stew.

I head for the exit trying to exude a fearlessness and a determination which I do not feel. I was prepared to deal with Harvey Claymore Junior but Harvey Senior is something else altogether.

CHAPTER SEVEN

For the past forty minutes I have been taking up space in a booth in the Astor coffee shop getting the fish-eye from my waitress as well as the matronly hostess with the beehive hairdo. I have run through two cups of coffee and one English muffin as well as my day's quota of patience. Then, just as I am ready to leave, I at last find myself sitting face to face with Anselm Forsythe III, allegedly one of the more brilliant attorneys to grace the New York legal scene. He has been recommended to me by dear dependable Bertha whose social connections in Gotham seem to be boundless. I did not ask her how and when she had come to know Forsthye III and she didn't volunteer it. Best a subject left alone although she admitted that it has been nearly twenty years since she's been in touch with him. Meeting here at the Astor is his idea. His offices, he tells me, are being repainted and redecorated by some high-priced Park Avenue interior decorator whose name I probably should know but don't.

His appearance matches his name. Expensive Brooks Brothers suit, gold rimmed Granny glasses, thinning hair, a pale and blood-less complexion and a patrician nose which he stares down, his gaze fixed on me. I put his age at a shade over fifty.

"You are Bertha Bowles partner?" he asks.

"I am," I say.

"Lovely woman, Bertha," he says. "She brightened many a day for me when I most needed it." He thinks about that for a moment and then snaps back to Planet Earth. "And so, what may I do for you, Mr. Bernardi? I understand your plight is most urgent."

"It is," I say. "A good friend is being held by the police as a material witness to a murder. She can identify the killer but the police have no idea who he is or where to find him. There is, in fact, no guarantee that they will ever locate him. I don't believe that under these circumstances they can continue to hold her. You're the lawyer. You tell me.

He sniffs quietly as he nods in agreement.

"In most instances you would be absolutely correct," he says. "I take it she's not an accomplice, anything like that."

"She is not," I say. "My sole interest in meeting with you, Mr. Forsythe, is to get her released. Locking her up is absurd."

"I quite agree," Forsythe says. "Given the circumstances you have described it should be a simple matter to have her released on her own recognizance or in your custody. You are aware of my fee schedule?"

"It's not a problem."

"Excellent," he smiles. "Now, tell me about the murder."

I relate the facts as best I can and he seems intrigued by the idea of a brazen police impersonator committing the act in the rear of a police station. But when I get around to mentioning Harvey Claymore Junior, his expression morphs from intrigue to disbelief.

"Young Claymore, you say?" he asks.

"Yes."

"Ahhh," he says thoughfully.

"You know him?"

"I'm acquainted with the family. "

Ahhh, I think to myself, also thoughtfully.

"You are quite sure young Claymore is involved here?" Forsythe asks.

"Quite," I say.

"So hard to believe, " he says. "A bright young man with a glowing future ahead of him. It strains credulity."

He's politely calling me a liar. I try to ignore it.

"Nevertheless," I say.

"Yes, nevertheless," he echoes. "Well, I shall have to look into this right away." He stands, his hand outstretched, I recognize the bum's rush when I see it. I stand and we shake. "I'll be in touch with the authorities to get the details and I will get back to you. I'm almost positive I can be of service to you."

In a pig's eye, I think. "I have your particulars, Mr. Bernardi, and I will be in touch." His smile is as sweet as Log Cabin syrup and twice as sticky. He turns on his heel and hurries away, leaving me to deal with a three-fifty check. I feel so bad for my waitress I drop a ten dollar bill on the table before I leave and head back to my room.

This is a depressing turn of events. A few minutes ago he was ready to collect a fee which rivals the New York City budget. However the mention of the name Claymore has cast me into the role of leperous intruder. Horvath is right. The Claymore tentacles run long and deep.

It's nearly noon when I put in a call to Toby Krantrz at the production office and apologize for missing the dailies the night before. I promise to be on hand this evening. Six o'clock. Yes, I have the name and address of the hotel. Before he hangs up Toby tells me where they are shooting this afternoon and also that Harold Hecht is back in town and anxious to get together with me. This is not happy news. My juggling act is about to get more difficult.

Almost immediately after I hang up, my phone rings. It's the hotel operator. While I was talking to Toby, John Crosby returned my call. I had called the Trib offices early this morning and left a message asking John to phone me. I dial the paper and pretty soon I've got him on the line.

"Welcome back to New York, Sergeant," he says to me. "Vacation or here on business?"

"Business, Captain."

"Still beating the drum for Jack Warner's third rate movies?"

"I left Jack ten months ago. I'm on my own now, partners with a very sharp lady named Bertha Bowles."

He laughs.

"My God, Joe, how is old Bertha? I haven't seen or heard from her in ages."

I'm floored. Is there anybody that 'old Bertha' DOESN'T know in this city?

"Bertha and I are both doing well, John."

"How long are you going to be in town?" he asks.

"At least four or five days. How about dinner some place outrageously expensive? On me, of course."

"Absolutely. Tonight's bad. So's tomorrow. What about Friday evening? Mary's got her art class at NYU and I'll be at loose ends."

"Friday for sure," I say. "I'll get back to you with a time and place."

"Can't wait, Sarge," he says.

"Same here, Captain."

I hang up and go into the bathroom where I throw a lot of cold water on my face and carefully comb my hair. With Hecht in town I decide I'd better make an appearance at the location to prove I'm involved. Besides I need to find a lawyer quick. Not some Park Avenue swell who wants to stay on Harvey Claymore's good side but a knuckles and knees guy who won't be afraid to mix it up. I suspect Tony Krantz who is a native New Yorker might know just the guy.

I'm heading for the door when my phone rings. I stop to answer it.

"Mr. Bernardi?"

"Yes?"

"This is Harvey Claymore."

I freeze in place.

"Harvey the younger?" I ask cautiously.

"That's right. I understand you've been running all over town asking questions about me."

"Not exactly," I say.

"It's okay. I understand you're a good friend of that poor girl they've got locked up in the courts building. I don't blame you for being upset. She went through a terrible ordeal."

"Not half as bad as the one Daphne Gennaro went through," I say.

"True enough," he says. "I thought we might have lunch."

"Well, I—"

"You have questions. I might be able to answer some of them."

"Maybe you can," I say.

"I'm in the lobby. Why don't you join me?"

"Sure. I'll be right down," I say and hang up.

I'm in the elevator on the way to the lobby, staring up at the descending numbers, when a thought hits me. How did Harvey Claymore Junior know that I was staying at the Hotel Astor? The visage of Anselm Forsythe III pops into my mind. I look down at my feet to see if I am standing in quicksand. Not yet.

I spot him immediately. The blonde hair, the watery grey eyes, the weak chin. He looks a lot like Dan Duryea but without the charm. His eyes fall on me as mine fall on him. He approaches tentatively.

"Mr. Bernardi?"

"Mr. Claymore?" I say in return.

He puts out his hand. We shake. It's like gripping a squid.

"I took the liberty of booking a table at the Carnegie Deli. I trust that meets with your approval."

"Sure," I say.

"My car's outside," he says and he starts to lead me across the lobby.

Harvey's car is a new Cadillac stretch limo. His driver's dressed in black and wears one if those funny little visored hats. His name is Franco and there is a noticeable bulge under his left arm pit. Obviously, Franco has been hired for more than his driving skills. We slip into the rear seat and Franco pulls away from the curb.

The Carnegie Deli, located next to Carnegie Hall, is two full blocks away from the Hotel Astor. A one-legged man on crutches could get there faster than we will by the time Franco has made several turns, avoided a one way street and a "No Left Turn" sign, been stopped at two red lights and sat overheating, waiting for lunchtime pedestrians to cross against the light at every intersection. Eventually we pull up at the front entrance and pile out. If anyone is impressed by our wheels, they give no sign of it. We walk inside and the maitre'd delicatessen beams broadly in welcome as Harvey approaches. He grabs two menus and leads us toward the rear and a corner booth at which a solitary older man is sitting, reading the front page of today's Wall Street Journal. As we approach the old man looks up and I need not be introduced to know who this is. The same watery eyes, the same weak chin, I am about to break bread with Harvey Claymore Senior.

Harvey Junior and I sit and we get the introductions out of the way. Senior is eyeing me analytically even as he keeps a polite smile plastered on his lips. He asks the usual questions. Am I here on vacation or business? How do I like the weather? Have I visited the Statue of Liberty yet? I tell him I'm not exactly a tourist and I'm here on company business. When he asks what kind of business, I tell him it's confidential. The less Senior knows about me and my affairs the better. The waiter comes by to take our order. When he gets to me, I ask him if the roast beef is rare. He gives me a look and says some is and some isn't but maybe I'd like to come in the kitchen and see for myself. This is when I remember that treating the customers rudely is a tradition at the Carnegie. I have to laugh. I switch to kreplach soup and a toasted onion bagel with a schmear of cream cheese. The waiter writes it down deadpan and says, "Funny, you don't look Jewish." He walks off as I shake my head in amusement. These guys have their routines down pat.

The levity over with, Harvey Senior gets down to business.

"I understand you have been asking questions about me and my son," he says.

"No, sir," I say, "just about your son."

"What concerns Harvey Junior concerns me, Mr. Bernardi," the old man says. He looks at Junior. "And where's your brother? He was supposed to be here."

"He's in Connecticut." Junior says.

Senior shakes his head in annoyance. "Schmuck," he mutters under his breath. He looks at me. "We are a close knit family, Mr. Bernardi, or at least we used to be. One for all, all for one. My youngest Biff should have been here to meet you and to support his brother. Instead he is off at a place called Lime Rock talking to people about building a car racing stadium in the middle of nowhere. Real estate, it seems, is too dull for him. He has to get mixed up with these southern rednecks and Wop grease monkeys. No offense intended."

I could say 'None taken' but I don't. This guy is a petty tyrant who loves pushing people around and it's my guess, after only ten minutes of idle conversation with the man, that Harvey Senior saves the best of his cruelty for his two sons.

For the third time since we sat down I look over at a nearby table where a solitary man is sitting nursing a cup of coffee. He's a big guy with a squarish lined face and short cropped steel-grey hair. His suit is ill fitting but even an expert tailor couldn't help him hide the gun he is carrying close to his left armpit. I notice that even though the room is jammed and people are waiting in the foyer, no one approaches the man to either order lunch or drink his coffee and give up the table. The other thing I notice is that every time I look in his direction he is carefully watching the three of us.

I lean in close to Harvey Senior.

"The gentleman at the nearby table. Does he have a problem with you, or maybe vice versa?"

Senior follows my gaze.

"None I know of," he says.

"He's carrying a gun," I say, "and he seems much too interested in this table."

"As he should," Senior says. "Mr. Fallon is my director of security. Where I go, he goes. I am a wealthy man with my share of enemies, Mr. Bernardi. I take precautions."

I nod. "Your security chief looks formidable," I say.

"Believe me, he is," Senior replies.

"Well, now," I say, "shall we talk about Daphne Gennaro, Mr.Claymore?"

He forces a sympathetic look.

"An unfortunate young woman," he says. "To suffer such a violent end, my heart grieves for her."

"And the baby, of course. We mustn't forget your son's child." I say.

His eyes get a little flinty. He may have thought I was going to be polite to him the way most people are. Now he realizes he was wrong.

"I have heard the rumor that she was pregnant, Even if that were true, it's unproven that the child was fathered by my boy."

"Of course. The autopsy will prove or disprove pregnancy and it's my understandng that various blood tests can be administered to confirm paternity."

"I've heard that," Senior says, "but in this case, I'm not sure there's anything to be gained by going through the time consuming procedure required."

"Oh, I doubt the police would agree," I say.

"We'll see," the old man says with a cold smile. Suddenly the smile fades and he freezes, the color draining from his face. He fumbles for his shirt pocket and takes out a tiny little bottle containing even tinier pills. He struggles to uncap it. Out of the corner of my eye I see Fallon on his feet and hurrying in our direction.

"Pop," Junior says anxiously, reaching for the bottle.

"I'm okay," Senior says.

"You're not okay," Fallon says, taking the bottle from Junior and uncapping it. He extracts a tiny pill. "Open." Senior opens wide and Fallon puts the pill on his employer's tongue. "Under your tongue, sir. Let it dissolve."

We watch as the old man closes his mouth and stares straight ahead. Junior looks at me and taps himself on his chest where his heart would be. I nod in understanding. After a minute or so Harvey Senior's color returns.

"You look better, Pop," Junior says.

"I'll be all right " he says, looking up at Fallon. "I'm okay now, Abe. You can go back to your table." Fallon nods and walks back to his cold cup of coffee.

Harvey Claymore Senior looks at me. His voice becomes quieter now, lacking energy. "We were discussing the mad man who shot the young woman. It's my belief, Mr. Bernardi, that he is some deranged person from her past, someone from the days when she worked for the so-called escort service."

"I'm not sure how a man like that would know that Miss Gennaro had been locked up in a cell in the rear of the Ninth Precinct."

"Stalking, Mr. Bernardi. Stalking. She was being followed by an obsessed former lover or client. You certainly cannot suspect my son. Your friend, Miss Johnson, gave an accurate description to the police. A sketch artist created a likeness which is being distributed all over the city. The killer looks nothing like my son."

"Then you've seen a copy of the sketch."

"A precinct captain who is a close friend had a patrol car drop it off at my office this morning." If I hadn't already been impressed, this was meant to seal the deal.

I smile politely.

"Well, I'm not surprised there's no likeness," I say. "In the unlikely event that he is somehow involved, I wouldn't expect your son to personally get his hands bloodied."

I look over at Junior who has not said one word of opposition or contradiction since we sat down at the table. In the presence of his father he has become mute. This only confirms my belief that he is a spineless weasel.

The old man is talking. I give him my attention.

"Anselm Forsythe, also a close friend, was good enough to call me this morning and tell me of your predicament with Miss Johnson. Frankly he wanted to help you but out of loyalty to me, he felt he had to check first to see if there was any conflict of interest. I assured him there wasn't. In any case, if you will re-connect with him, he will see that Miss Johnson is free to leave, perhaps as early as this evening."

'Very thoughtful of him and of you as well, Mr. Claymore."

He shrugs humbly. Noblesse oblige.

"And I will be responsible for his fee as well," Senior says.

"That won't be necessary," I say.

"The amount is substantial," he says.

"I know," I say laconically, "but the pound sterling upticked eight points this morning and I'm well positioned for a long term gain." I have only a vague idea what I just said but it's the kind of thing Jack Warner would spout off when he'd made a killing.

"As you wish," Senior says with a shrug.

After that it's a speed lunch. Business out of the way, Senior has places to go and things to do. Because I spent my late teen years working the petroleum fields in Texas I know a lot of the jargon and I give him the impression I am an oil baron with myriad interests. I can't get him to talk about himself but he does rag at great length on his younger son, Biff, who is an ungrateful wastrel with no appreciation for money, a total lack of discipline and only grudging respect for the man who pays his bills. The more he rails, the more it becomes obvious that bad boy Biff is the old man's favorite and dull and steady Harvey Junior might as well not even exist. If there were a daughter around, I would say that this family closely resembles the Borgias.

As we are saying our goodbyes, I promise to get back to Anselm Forsythe III immediately. Junior offers me a ride back to the hotel but I tell him I can't spare the time and so I walk. Twelve minutes later I am in my room rummaging about in the yellow pages. I find what I am looking for under "Automobiles- Rentals". For what I have in mind, a yellow cab simply will not do.

CHAPTER EIGHT

he clock on the wall reads 7:22 and not only am I running out of patience but my butt is getting sorer with every passing minute. The hard wooden benches in the visitor's waiting room at the courthouse were not manufactured with creature comfort in mind. I stand and start to pace. Let my feet feel the brunt of the boredom for a while.

I have spent a busy day. Upon returning to the hotel I made arrangements to rent a car for the rest of my stay in the city. Then I phoned Anselm Forsythe III who was expecting my call. He was confident that he'd get Alice (Bunny) released this evening shortly after six o'clock. I told him I'd meet him at the courthouse building at six. I called the "Marty" production office. Toby was at the location but I spoke with Ruby, telling her I was very disappointed I was going to once again miss dailies this evening but gave her my solemn word I would show up tomorrow. Ruby said she, too, was disappointed that she wouldn't be seeing me tonight. I think I heard a coquettish little flirtation buried in all that Brooklynese and it suddenly occured to me that Ruby might have designs on me. Ridiculous. I'm old enough to be her, well, older brother. I tried to overlook the fact that she might be impressed by my mature bearing, my veneer of sophistication and my Italian good looks. Well, yes,

I can see how she might be drawn to me in a casual sort of a way but viewed realistically, it really is an absurd idea. Nevertheless, I made a note to get a haircut tomorrow and to have the hotel clean and press my spiffy navy blue blazer, the one that gives me that devil-may-care 'Tyrone Power' look.

At three I left the hotel to pick up my rental car. After that a quick visit to Macy's for a few minutes shopping and then a stop at the bank to cash a check on the theory that when you need flexibility, you can never have too many greenbacks in your pocket. I did this because the moment Harvey Claymore Senior volunteered to help me spring Bunny from jail, I felt the deadly chill of betrayal shoot up my back. True, someone—maybe someone hired by a Claymore—was able to get to Daphne Genarro at the Ninth Precinct but security at the Municipal Court Building is something else altogether. In the killer's mind it is probably far better to have her out on the street where she will present a much easier target. I vow to do my best to make sure that doesn't happen.

"Expecting twins?"

I stop pacing and turn at the sound of Horvath's voice. He's standing in the open doorway to the waiting room, a wry smile on his face.

"I missed my morning jog," I lie since I have never willingly jogged for exercise in my life.

"You're making a mistake, you know," he says to me.

"So you've told me."

He lights up a cigarette as he comes into the room and tosses the dead match into an ashtray already overflowing with butts.

"Are you planning to stay by her side twenty-four hours a day?"

"If need be," I say.

"And if you do, is that any guarantee this nutcase won't get to her and also to you while he's at it. Or maybe you're impervious to bullets."

"Better to be free and able to run than be trapped in a steel cage."

"Aren't you a little curious to why Claymore's pet lawyer so quickly changed his mind about helping you?"

"Following orders?"

"Something like that. Somebody buys a hit on Junior's pregnant girlfriend, probably Junior himself though I wouldn't rule out the old man, and then conveniently the family helps spring the only eyewitness from the safety of the municipal courthouse building into the protective embrace of an unarmed press agent. And by the way, Bernardi, you are unarmed, aren't you?"

"At the moment," I say.

"Well, just as a point of information, it is illegal to carry a handgun in this city without a permit."

"I see. And how does one go about getting a permit?"

"One doesn't."

"And the penalty for carrying without a permit?" I ask.

"Death by hanging," Horvath says, reviving that same wry smile.

"I'll keep that in mind," I say.

"Do that," he says reaching into his pocket and taking out one of his cards which he hands to me. "If and when you get tired of playing Dick Tracy, give me a call. My home phone's on the back."

"I can take care of myself, Sergeant," I tell him.

"I'm sure you can," he says, "but here's my problem. If anything happens to you I'm going to have to fill out enough paperwork to fill a good sized trash barrel and that is something I don't look forward to."

"I'll do my best to stay safe," I say.

Horvath smiles.

"I feel better already," he says.

Just then I look toward the doorway as Bunny enters accompanied by Forsythe. She's dressed plainly in civilian clothes and she doesn't look much better than she did when I first saw her curled up on her cell cot.

I go to her and take her hands in mine. I'd like to embrace her but I'm still not sure where I fit in. She smiles at me. It's a smile of thanks and it's a start.

"Nice work, counselor," Horvath says as he heads for the door. "Who signed your writ? Judge Battaglia? Must have been a tough call for him, considering he has to check with Claymore every time he needs to blow his nose." Sarcasm drips from every syllable.

"Find your killer, Sergeant, and the lady returns to custody. But nothing in the code says the police can keep someone locked up indefinitely while they flounder around in an inept investigation."

Horvath forces a smile and goes to the door. He looks back at me. "Remember, any time, day or night." And he leaves.

Forsythe watches him go. "A good officer," he says, "but in this case, he has his priorities out of place." He smiles and stretches out his arm toward the doorway. "Shall we go?" he says. "My car is right outside."

The sun is starting to lower itself below the horizon to the west when we step outside. The temperature is brisk, typical of mid-September in New York. A Lincoln town car is parked at curbside with Forsythe's driver standing at the ready. "If you don't mind, Mr. Forsythe," I say, "Alice and I are going to grab a cab back to the hotel."

"It's no trouble," he says.

I smile politely.

"I'm sure it's not," I say, "but we have a lot to catch up on. We could use a little privacy."

Forsythe licks his lips and I think I see a flicker of uncertainty in his eyes. For whatever reason this decision is not sitting well.

"Surely that can wait until you are back at the hotel." he says.

"No, it can't," I say sharply.

"But Mr. Claymore—." He stops short.

"Mr. Claymore what?" I say even more sharply.

"Nothing," he says after a hesitation.

"Mr. Claymore what?" I'm not letting him off the hook.

Finally he says, "Mr. Claymore wishes you to know he was happy to help out in this situation."

"Fine. Tell him we're grateful," I say to him as I take Bunny by the arm and hustle her toward the taxi stand halfway down the block. Bunny reads my grim expression.

"What's wrong?" she asks.

"Maybe nothing," I say, "but I wouldn't bet your life on it."

We hop into the back of the first cab in line. When the cabbie asks where to, I tell him to just drive. As we pull away from the curb, I scrunch around and look out the rear window into the gathering dusk. Forsythe is slowly getting into his car and obviously has no intention of following us. Not so the black and ivory Chevy Bel Air that was parked across the street from the courthouse. It makes a quick U-turn in the middle of the street, nearly colliding with a laundry van, and positions itself maybe forty yards behind us.

"Damn!" I say, loud enough for our driver to hear. "It's Ralph."

Bunny gives me a puzzled look but I signal her to silence and then lean forward.

"Driver," I say, "we have a problem. See that car behind us?"

"Yeah, I seen him," the driver says without turning his head. "Dumb son of a bitch almost took out that laundry truck."

"Me and the wife just got married and the guy back there is her ex-boyfriend, crazy as a loon. Any chance you could lose the guy. There's a twenty dollar tip in it for you."

"For twenty bucks, I'll run him into the river for you," the cabbie laughs and hits the gas. "Hang on."

We hang on and Wally, that's our driver, scoots down one alley after another, taking turns on two wheels and checking every three or four seconds to make sure his horn is still working. Finally after one harrowing maneuver involving a moving van and a motorcycle he pulls in line at a cab stand behind four other yellow cabs.

"Duck down!" he says as he opens his door and hops out carrying a copy of today's newspaper. He opens it up and leans against the cab's hood, languidly picking his teeth with a toothpick and reading the front page in the fading light. A few seconds later the Bel Air comes roaring up the street, flies by to the intersection ahead and after a moment's pause, turns left, burning rubber in the process. We remain like that for a good five minutes before Wally gets back behind the wheel.

"They're gone," he announces. "Where to?"

I give him the address and twelve minutes later we pull up to Cargill's Parking Garage on West 51st Street. I hand Wally a fifty dollar bill.

"You never saw me and the missus and you sure don't remember where you took us," I say.

"You got that right, pal," Wally says pocketing the fifty. I watch as he drives off.

"I thought we were going to the hotel," Bunny says.

"Change of plans," I tell her. "I'll explain on the way."

"On the way where?" she asks.

I don't answer but walk over to the cashier's office where I surrender my ticket. A short time later the new Ford Victoria hardtop I'd rented earlier comes down on the elevator. Bunny gets in the passenger side and I slip behind the wheel. I pull into traffic and head for the West Side Highway where I turn onto a northbound ramp and drive toward the Bronx.

"You hungry?" I ask her. "We could stop to eat."

"I'm fine," she says. "Where are we going?"

"White Plains," I tell her.

I can feel her looking over at me. I keep my eyes on the road. It's dark now. Traffic is heavy.

"You don't have to do this," she says.

"You need a place to hide out until the cops catch up with this maniac. Two birds, one stone."

"It's too much," she says. "I can't let you do it."

"You've got no choice, Bunny. It's arranged. You're checking in under an assumed name. In the trunk I have a suitcase filled with clothes. I guessed at sizes but I'm pretty close. For the next sixty days you're an up and coming actress with a drinking problem. You'll be safe because the people at the hospital will have no idea who you really are."

She has taken it all in. Now she slumps down in her seat and stares out her window at the lights of Manhattan, a city she once held in the palm of her hand. How she let it slip away I don't know. I've never asked her and never will. Maybe someday she'll tell me.

She sits in silence for the longest time. I grant her quietude. If she wants to talk she will but I won't press her. The windshield starts to mist up. It's started to rain. Not heavy. Just a light drizzle, I flip on the wipers. The road starts to turn a silvery wet ahead of me.

"I wanted to come back, Joe. I really did. But I couldn't," she says after a while.

"Okay," I say.

"I had my reasons."

"I'm sure you did."

The Cross Bronx Expressway looms up ahead. I turn onto it, heading east, then get off at the exit for the White Plains Post Road and start north.

"Life's so damned hard, Joe. Why does life have to be so damned hard?"

"I don't know, Bunny. It's not always hard. There are good times. We had good times."

"Yes," she says and falls back into silence.

Slap,slap,slap. The wipers go back and forth fighting harder now to keep the windshield clear. The rain is more persistent. The roadway is soaked and glistening and here and there water splashes up where I run through a rut or a depression.

"That could have been me," she says.

"What?"

"Daphne. That could have been me. The things I did, the people I hung around with, the booze. Every night, always the same. I hated it. I felt worthless and ashamed, Joe. I hated it but I couldn't live without it. Even when I tried to stop, I found myself drowning in the thought of it. Needing it. So weak. So pitiful. Disgusting."

"But you stopped, Bunny. You did manage to stop. Pat said you were coming up on six months."

"Nothing. Six months is nothing. I quit twice before and then went back. You don't know until you've been there, Joe. Every morning, every evening that's all you can think about. One drink. Just one. It can't hurt. Not just one. Thats what you keep telling yourself and deep down you know it's a god damned lie."

I take a quick glance over at her. Tears are trickling down her cheeks.

"I'm suffocating, Joe. I can't breathe. I just want my life back. Is that so much to ask?"

I have no answer for that except a vacuous platitude so I keep my mouth shut. I look over again. She's closed her eyes looking to shut out her demons. I let her be.

Twenty minutes later I turn left at the high chain link fence and follow it down to the middle of the block where I find the entrance to the hospital. I turn in and drive up to the security booth with its black and white striped barrier arm. A uniformed guard with clipboard in hand steps out to greet us. Even before he asks, he knows who we are. Smith-Lerner Hospital doesn't normally entertain admissions at this hour of the night but I've convinced them to make an exception considering the very hush-hush circumstances involved. The guard directs us to Visitor Parking next to the main entrance and says he will notify Dr. Anders that we have arrived.

Dorothea Anders is a tall, thin bird like woman in her mid to late 50's and when she talks her head bobs a lot and her hands flutter in all directions. She approaches with hand outstretched, peering at me through thick rimless glasses that make her eyes seem bigger than they really are.

"So nice to meet you, Mr. Bernardi," she says, "and so nice that we will be able to help you and—"

I put my hand up to silence her.

"For the duration of her stay, the young lady will be known by the name Melanie Morgan. I hope you understand, Doctor, the gossip columnists would sell their souls to learn that this rising Hollywood star is here being treated for her addiction. They are jackals, Doctor, unprincipled jackals without compassion."

"Yes, yes, I understand," she says, taking Bunny's hand. "Poor child, you will be safe here with us."

"Thank you," Bunny says gratefully, playing her part to the hilt.

"And I promise you, we will wean you from the clutches of demon alcohol. Trust in us and trust in God, that is all we ask."

"I will," she says taking the doctor's hand and squeezing it.

I reach in my jacket pocket for a bulky envelope and hand it to Dr. Anders.

"This will cover your fee for the sixty-day treatment. I've also enclosed an additional five hundred dollars to pay for any unexpected incidental expenses Miss Morgan may encounter."

"Very good," Anders says. "Now considering the hour I think we should get Miss Morgan settled in. Nurse Dowd will show you to your room, dear, and we can deal with the paperwork tomorrow."

"Doctor," I say, '"there is no paperwork. Remember?"

"Oh, yes, of course," she says, hands continuing to flutter.

Bunny turns to me and suddenly she is in my arms and holding me close. She is trembling and I can feel her heart beating against my chest. And then just as quickly she slips away from me and I watch as she walks away, suitcase in hand, accompanied by Nurse Dowd. I ache for her. She seems small, though she isn't. She appears thin and frail and she is. There is something in the way she carries herself that tells me she is afraid. She has endured a lot. This may be her last chance and I'm pretty sure she knows it. If she fails here she will face an ugly and destructive future that has but one ending. I would pray for her but I don't know how. The most I can offer her is hope. Maybe it'll be enough.

I turn to Dr. Anders and ask her if I can use her phone. I have an important call to make before I head back to the city.

CHAPTER NINE

find Horvath in the coffee shop nursing a cup of coffee and nibbling an English muffin. It's not yet ten o'clock. I made record time getting here from the hospital. Horvath looks up as I slide into the booth across from him.

"This had better be good," he says. "My wife despises you and she hasn't even met you."

"This IS good and tomorrow morning I'll send your wife a dozen roses."

"She has allergies. Send her a Whitman's Sampler."

"Done," I say.

"So where is Johnson? Up in the room?"

"She's safe."

"What's that supposed to mean?"

"It means, she's safe."

"You've stashed her someplace. Where?"

"Can't tell you."

"What do you mean, you can't tell me? I'm a police officer."

"And probably a pretty good one, but I can't tell you."

"You mean, you won't tell me."

"That's right," I say with more than a little annoyance. "I know where she is. Nobody else. That's how I can be sure she'll be safe.

Yesterday when I left the courthouse, we were followed and if we hadn't been able to shake the bastards, they'd have found out where I was taking her. Now do you understand why I'm being so secretive?"

A long silence.,

"Those were my bastards," Horvath says finally.

"What?"

"They were police officers. You didn't really think I was going to let you waltz out of the courthouse with that woman without keeping tabs on you, did you. Mr. Bernardi?"

"I don't need a keeper," I say.

"The hell you don't," Horvath says. Then, "Oh, forget it," he says in disgust, "I'm wasting my time here."

He starts to get up.

"Do you want to catch this son of a bitch or don't you?" I ask.

Horvath hesitates.

"I suppose you've got some goddamned fool proof scheme up your sleeve."

"Maybe not foolproof but pretty good," I say. "I don't think it would take much to convince our killer that Bunny is upstairs in my room."

"Who?"

"Bunny. That's her name. Bunny. And if the killer thinks she's up there, he may make a try for her. Otherwise why go to all the trouble of getting her out of jail?"

Horvath sits back down.

"Correct me if I'm wrong but isn't old man Claymore the one who paved the way for her to get out of jail?"

"That's right," I say. "He was even happy to supply me with a lawyer who seemed very annoyed that I refused to accept a ride from him away from the jailhouse. Wonder where he was planning to take us?"

"So you're accusing Claymore and Forsythe of hiring someone—"

"I'm not accusing anybody of anything. I just find their cooperation odd to say the least."

"You know what you're suggesting."

"Of course I do. I could very well be wrong, Sarge, but what if I'm not?"

Horvath sits quietly for a few moments., sifting through it.

"Okay. Say you're right. Where do I fit in?"

"You supply me with a credible double, someone who could pass for Bunny if you don't look too closely."

"And?"

"And I check her in at the desk as my wife for all the world to see and then we go up to our room. We create the illusion that we're in for the night and with that fiction set in stone and the trap well baited, we sit back and wait."

He shakes his head.

"It'll never work."

"And how much headway are you making at your end? Look, Sergeant, I know one thing for sure. We can't deal with this guy on his timetable or play by his rules. We need to lure him out of his rathole and if he's got the guts to commit murder in a police station, a hotel room certainly isn't going to scare him off."

Horvath stares at me, mulling it over, weighing the alternatives. "I need to make a phone call," he says as he slides out of the booth. I watch as he walks over to a bank of pay phones against a far wall and starts to make a call. Fifteen minutes later he returns to the booth.

"Her name is Vicki Caputo. She'll be here by eleven. I told her to wear her civvies, a bandana on her head and dark glasses. She was about to go off shift but when I told her what it was all about, she jumped at the chance."

"Can she handle it?" I ask.

Horvath laughs.

"She's got ten years in, she's smart and she's fearless and a day when she doesn't throw some worthless sack of crap into a jail cell is a day wasted."

"I love her already," I say.

"And if you come on to her, you won't be able to walk for a week."

"I'll remember that," I say.

"Oh, and one other thing. My wife says forget Whitmans. She prefers Ghiardelli."

I say I'll remember that, too.

At precisely eleven o'clock, she comes sauntering into the Astor lobby, dressed as advertised. She is slim and the right height and coloring and if I didn't know better, from a distance I could easily mistake her for Bunny.

I approach her, arms extended to give her a welcoming hug.

"Thanks for coming, Miss Caputo," I whisper in her ear.

"Watch your hands, buster," she whispers back as she extricates herself from my grasp. "Where's the Sergeant?" I tell her that Horvath is up on the ninth floor having checked into a room three doors down from mine. I say I'll explain everything when we're safely upstairs.

We walk over to the front desk and go through the rigamarole of having her added to the room as my wife. I use this as an excuse to make a scene regarding room charges so that I can draw attention to us. I haven't seen anyone hanging around the lobby who looks remotely like the police sketch of the killer but I'm taking no chances. He may not be operating alone.

We go upstairs to my room. call Horvath and he joins us. We go over the plan one more time for Vicki's benefit. She and I will be in the room, at least one of us awake at all times. If someone comes to the door and wants to gain entry—room service, building maintenance, housekeeping—we immediately ring up Horvath's room. He steps out into the corridor and checks out whoever's at our door. The same applies if we hear someone trying to tamper with the door lock. Vicki is armed with a snub-nosed.38 and she guarantees she knows how to use it. If Daphne Gennaro's killer shows up looking for Bunny, he's going to find a lot more than he bargained for.

Vicki stretches out in the bed, propped up by two pillows. Her eyes are wide open. Her pistol sits on the night stand beside her. I'm settled in on the small sofa by the window. It's not yet midnight and the lights of the city still blaze brightly from below. This really is magical place, I think. The city where I work deals in illusion. New York is the real deal, the heartbeat of America, the engine of its prosperity, a welcoming Mecca for the past century to the downtrodden of Europe, the Irish and the Italians, the Germans and the Swedes, the Poles and the Russians all of whom passed through on the way to a better life than the one they left behind. It is also a cruel city. If you cannot succeed, it casts you aside, destroying you the way it tried to destroy Bunny. Thinking back I realize she never had a chance. She had the talent but she didn't have the shell. Too trusting, too accomodating, too vulnerable. In the end the city spit her out.

I shift positions. I'm starting to get drowsy and I know I can't. I check out the mini-bar and grab a Hershey with almonds (20c) and a Coca-Cola (25c) to get some caffeine into my system. I check with Vicki. She passes. At these prices it's a good thing.

By three o'clock nothing has happened. The couple above us played bouncy-bouncy on their bed for a few minutes and a couple of drunks came laughing and stumbling down the hallway around two-thirty. Otherwise, quiet.

Six o'clock finally comes. Our killer has not. The first rays of the morning sun are peering through the buildings to the east. Vicki is still wide awake. I'm positive she never once closed her eyes. I can't say the same for me. Horvath rings us up at seven and says he's coming over. When he arrives I apologize profusely to both of them. I was certain the killer would make a try. Horvath tells me not to fret it. It was a good idea or he wouldn't have gone along.

He looks at Vicki. "Maybe he wants to catch you alone. You game for one more day?"

"Why not?" she says, opening the .38 and double checking the load. She spins the cylinder and then slams it back into position.

Horvath picks up the phone, dials headquarters, and asks for somebody named Feeney. When he comes on the line, Horvath speaks to him quietly.

"You must be hungry," I say to Vicki.

"I'll live," she says.

"Before we go we'll order room service," I say.

"Sure, that'll be nice." She cocks her head at me with a curious smile. "So who is she? Your girlfriend?"

"Used to be."

She nods.

"Gotta be rough, seeing her friend get blown away like that and then this gorilla aiming his friggin' gun at her."

"She'll be okay," I say.

"She'll be okay if we catch this creep. We get him or he gets her, that's what it comes down to because he's not going to quit and neither are we. You get that, don't you, sir?"

"Yes, Vicki," I say, "I get that."

I like her. A great combination of sharp and blunt. Sharp mind, blunt talk. Face reality. Tell it like it is. I see why Horvath brought her into this. Law enforcement could use a lot more just like her.

Horvath gets off the phone and tells us that Detective Al Feeney will be here in a half hour to take over in the room down the hall. We order room service for Vicki while she takes a cold shower to clear out the cobwebs. The room service waiter is a young blond kid named Sven. We let him in and get Vicki organized. We make a point of telling Sven that Vicki will be staying in all day and is not to be disturbed. I'll pass this same message on to the desk clerk before I leave the hotel. I don't like leaving Vicki like this but Horvath has persuaded me that our only chance at luring the killer into our web is to convince him totally that Vicki is alone and vulnerable.

At ten o'clock I walk out of the Astor into the sunlight. It looks to be a gorgeous day. The temperature has climbed to the high 70's and a lot of businessmen are walking around with their suit jackets slung over their shoulders. My thoughts are with Vicki and Al Feeney up there on the ninth floor and I feel impotent. I want to be there with them but I know I can't and so I try to force them from my mind. Besides I have an agenda of my own this morning and it has less to do with the paid killer who took Daphne Gennaro's life than the man who hired him. As I start to cross the street, I notice a man who has been standing by the hotel entrance. He met my gaze when I first came out and now I see that he is continuing to watch me closely.

Across from the Astor is an open air newsstand and I pick up a copy of today's New York Times. I realize that I am hungry and when I spot a hole in the wall coffee shop halfway down the block, I decide to take ten minutes for a coffee and a bagel. It's then that I figure out I'm not only being watched, I'm being followed.

I enter the coffee shop and find myself a spot at the counter where I can watch the front door. The counterman takes my order and I open the paper to the real estate section, still keeping one eye on the entrance. After a few moments he steps inside and looks around. When his gaze falls on me, he stops looking and walks toward me.

He's a burly guy, not fat but heavy set, with wild untamed hair and a nose that's been broken more times than a gigolos's promises. He peers at me through black-rimmed heavy duty glasses as he sits in the stool next to me.

"I don't want any trouble," I say to him.

"Trouble? Why should I give you trouble?" he asks.

"Look, if you're one of Horvath's men I don't need you and if you work for Claymore I'm calling the cops."

He allows himself a faint smile.

"Don't do that on my account," he says.

"Who are you?" I ask, now puzzled.

"Paddy Chayefsky, Mr. Bernardi, and I may be pleased to meet you. That remains to be seen."

Paddy Chayefsky. I can hardly believe it. One of my idols. The man who wrote "Marty" as well as a dozen other top drawer television dramas.

I put out my hand.

"Joe Bernardi."

"I know," he says neglecting to shake.

"It's an honor to meet you," I say.

"You have a funny way of showing it, pal," Chayefsky says signalling to the counterman. "Coffee!" he calls to him. "I don't quite get you, Mr. Bernardi. I heard you'd be working with us on publicity. You show up on Wednesday, spend a couple of hours and then disappear. You're supposed to come for dailies but you didn't show. Next day, same thing. Here it is Friday, Harold is back from Los Angles and he asks me how it's workjng out with you and I tell him we're dealing with the Invisible Man. When I explain, he tells me to go look for you and find out what the hell is going on. "

"Yes, I'm sorry about that," I say. "I've been kind of distracted."

"Distracted? What's that supposed to mean? We've got a film here that all of us are sweating blood for. All of us, Mr. Bernardi, right down to the lens puller because we think we've got something very special on our hands. This is not just another low budget movie which is probably what you think."

"No, I—"

"It isn't always about big name stars and big special effects and technicolor and, what the hell is it? Stereophonic sound? Movies, the good ones, are about people. But maybe that's not the kind of picture you know how to promote."

Now I'm getting sore. Idol or no idol, I don't like being lectured to. "Look," I say, "I'm sorry. I'm wrong. I should be spending every day with the company and starting today I will."

Chayefsky stares at me hard as the counterman brings our coffee and my bagel.

"I've got no use for bullshitters," he says.

"I'll be there for dailies tonight. Six o'clock."

"You know where?"

"I know where."

"We'll be looking for you," he says as he gets up off his stool. "Coffee's on you," he says and he leaves. And of course, he's right. Either I'm working for this movie or I'm not. With all that's going on, maybe I should beg off. Bunny's my first priority. She has to be. Maybe I'll get lucky and we'll grab this guy today and put an end to my dilemma. Yes, that's it. I'll give it one more day and make a decision tomorrow. Tonight, the dailies. For sure.

I sip my coffee and resume looking at the real estate section of the morning Times. After about a minute of searching I find exactly what I'm looking for.

CHAPTER TEN

It's five minutes to three when I walk up to the entrance to 1750 Sixth Avenue. That's what New Yorkers call it. Tourists call it the Avenue of the Americas. It's an imposing building, twenty four stories high only three blocks north of Rockefeller Plaza. There is a discreet sign outside the main entrance notifying anyone interested that there is office space available. A phone number is prominently displayed. So is the name of the realty company: Claymore Properties.

I stride confidentally to the security desk. Josiah Smith here to meet with Harvey Claymore Jr., I tell him. He nods and directs me to the bank of elevators. Eleventh floor, he says. Mr. Claymore has already arrived. I take the first available elevator. Maybe I should be nervous but I'm not. I'm mostly irritated, torn between two conflicting duties, one to Bertha and the other to Bunny. I made this appointment shortly before lunch with Junior's secretary. I saw your ad in the Times, I told her. The office space in question sounds perfect for my needs. We must meet this afternoon. I'm flying to London this evening on business. No, I don't want to deal with Harvey Senior. I have been advised by my attorney to meet only with his son.

The elevator door opens and I step out into a deserted bare-bones hallway. Everything is painted white. The floor is cement, ready to be covered with wall to wall carpeting of the tenant's choosing. Glass double-doors face the elevators and I push through them into an equally unfinished office complex, a rabbit warren of corridors and cubicles and private offices that afford views of Sixth Avenue and 52nd Street. Again everything is white with recessed lighting everywhere. The Times ad listed the footage at 13,500 and I believe every inch of it. This has the potential be an awe inspiring suite of offices.

I hear voices and they are comng from an office at the end of the corridor I've stepped into. I recognize Junior's voice but not the other one. "Write the damned check! You have the authority. Just do it!"

Whoever he is he sounds both angry and desperate.

"No. Dad would skin me alive as soon as he realized what I'd done." Harvey Junior says.

"So what? He's already half dead. What's he going to do, Harv? Fire you? Disinherit you? He can't do that. You know it and so does he."

"He's not dead yet, Biff. He deserves a little respect."

Aha, Younger brother Biff. A sibling quarrel. I stop dead in my tracks hoping to hear more. "And since when did he show me anything but contempt?" Biff says.

"That's crap and you know it."

"For Christ's sake, Harv, write the damned check. Call it a loan, I'll sign a note. Anything. But I have to pony up four hundred and fifty thousand by the end of the month or they go ahead without me."

"Then let 'em go," Junior says angrily. "A racetrack in the middle of nowhere. You and your friends are out of your collective minds. You want the money, you go to Pop like a man and you ask him for it."

"Maybe I will."

"And maybe you won't, Biff. Maybe you won't."

"Well, fuck you!"

I press back against the wall as if that's going to make me invisible as Biff Claymore charges out of the office at the end of the corridor. He's considerably younger than his brother, maybe early twenties but he has the Claymore genes. He slows as he sees me and looks me up and and down. The cold rage in his eyes cannot be hidden.

"He's asking one-thirty-five but he'll he'll settle for a buck-ten. Don't let him fuck you over." Biff Claymore continues on toward the elevator well as I turn and start toward the open door of the office at the end of the hall.

The room is empty and unfurnished except for one large wooden desk at which Harvey Junior is sitting with his face in his hands. Atop the desk are various brochures, a legal pad, some pencils and pens and a telephone. I rap on the door jamb and he looks up. Inexplicably he doesn't seem to be pleased to see me.

"Go away, Bernardi. I have no time for you now. I'm waiting for a client."

I raise my hand with a smile.

"Present," I say.

He regards me with disgust.

"What's the big idea?" he asks.

"The big idea is to get you alone where we can talk without your father hovering around."

"You and I have nothing to talk about," he says getting up from his chair. His suit jacket has been draped over the back of the chair. Now he slips into it.

"I think we do. You could always talk to the police but that wouldn't be half as much fun."

He shrugs.

"They know where to find me. I have nothing to hide."

"The night she was killed, Daphne called you. What did you

two talk about?"

"I didn't talk to her."

"The phone company says different. The phone company says you chatted for almost three minutes."

"Not me," he says. "Biff answered the phone."

"Oh, your brother was visiting?"

"That's right."

"I didn't realize you two were so close."

"We had business to discuss. Family business and none of yours:"

"So she talked to Biff."

"That's right."

"She wanted you to come to the precinct and get her out of jail."

"Yes, she did."

"You never showed up."

"No, I didn't," Junior says.

"But you told her you would."

"No. Biff told her I would. Anything to shut her up and get her off the phone."

"And meanwhile, you're over at your father's townhouse having dinner and playing bridge until the wee hours of the morning. I mean, that is what you told the police, isn't it, Mr. Claymore?"

He shakes his head.

"That was my father's idea," he says. "He tells me my situation is less messy if I have a solid alibi."

"So you lie to the cops because your father thinks it's a good idea."

"He knew I had nothing to do with Daphne's death."

"And the couple you were playing bridge with?"

"The company's chief appraiser and his wife."

I laugh. "Oh, well, that's rock solid. And was there actually a bridge game?" I ask.

"There will have been, if necessary," Junior replies. "Anything else?"

"A few hours after this phone call you didn't take, a man with a gun shows up outside Daphne Gennaro's jail cell and damn near blows her head off."

"I don't know anything about that," Junior says.

"Really? And who do you think does?' I ask him.

"I don't know. Biff maybe, though I can't think why. Or my father. Yes, much more likely my father. He was having her followed, you know."

"No, I didn't know."

"Being ultra careful," Junior says bitterly. "We'd had our talk a few days ago. Get rid of the woman or get disinherited. It wasn't a long conversation."

"And you went along?"

"Sure."

"Even though she was carrying your child."

Junior shakes his head.

"She said she was carrying my child. Guys like me with plenty of money hear things like that a lot."

"The autopsy confirmed that she was pregnant," I tell him.

He looks at me sharply as if I'd dealt him a body blow.

After a moment he says, "Okay, so she was pregnant."

"If you'd known that for sure, would you stlll have had her killed?"

"I told you, I had nothing to do with that."

"You didn't hire someone to get rid of her, per your father's wishes?"

"No!" he says angrily. "Look, I was in love with Daphne but I wasn't going to throw away everything on a gesture when I knew my old man would be dead within a year. So maybe I turned my back on her temporarily. I wanted her back, I swear to God, and eventually I would have gotten her back but I couldn't do it while my father was alive. To him she was a whore and would never be anything else."

"And your father was having her followed?"

"Yes."

"By who?"

"I don't know."

"Did you ever meet him? See him?"

"No."

"Then how do you know she was being followed?"

"Because it's what he does. He'd done it before, with other women I'd known when I was younger."

I nod.

Just then the phone rings. Harvey Junior picks it up.

"Claymore Properties. Oh, yes, I was expecting your call." He swivels around putting his back to me but I still get the gist of the conversation. "No,no,I'm all set. I have a six o'clock reservation and I'll be able to stay until Sunday.... Yes, that's very generous.... I'm looking forward to the grand tour..... No, it'll be just me..... All right, I'll meet you in the lobby a little after nine o'clock... Till then."

He swings around and hangs up.

"Leaving town?" I ask.

"There's a hotel for sale in Atlantic City. A real dump just like the rest of the town but there's talk of legalizing gambling, maybe not right away but if and when it goes through, it'll be a bonanza, Vegas East. Can't miss and I can't wait." He says this with a fairly smug smile.

"And your father approves?"

"It's getting to the point where my father is no longer relevant."

The smile is gone. He says it coldly and I realize that I may have misjudged the man badly. He plays the role of obsequious son exceptionally well but behind all that toadying is unfettered ambition and a steely no-nonsense determination.

"I believe we're through here. Mr. Bernardi," Junior says as he

91

turns his attention back to his paperwork. I start out, then hesitate in the doorway and turn back to him.

"One last question, Mr. Claymore," I say.

"Goodbye, Mr, Bernardi, and don't bother to close the door as you leave."

"How short a leash has your father got Forsythe on?"

Harvey looks up at me sharply.

"I'm not sure I understand the question," he says.

"Sure, you do," I reply. "The day he managed to get Alice Johnson released from police custody, he did so on orders from your father. I also think he was under orders to bring Alice to your father, for what reason I don't know."

"Neither do I. Goodbye, Mr. Bernardi."

"Someone very close to me, someone whose opinion I value, recommended Forsythe to me as an able attorney. She had warned me she hadn't seen or heard from him in over twenty years but she assured me he was a bright and successful lawyer. My question to you, Harvey, is, what happened to him?"

A crooked smile appears on his face.

"Given my age I can hardy be expected to know what Anselm Forsythe was like twenty years ago. Maybe he was a modern day Darrow though I doubt it. I do know that fifteen years ago he went through a messy and costly divorce which took most of his assets and a second divorce five years later cost him whatever remained. He drank a lot then, more than he does now, and nobody wanted to retain him. Nobody but my father, that is, who put him on an annual retainer. You see my Dad needs total and unconditional loyalty and Forsythe played the perfect toady. No job too dirty, no task too loathsome. In the knuckles and knees game of real estate, my father plays dirty out of habit, Mr. Bernardi, and Forsythe has been, and stlll is, his enforcer. Any other questions?"

Still that crooked smile. I shrug and return it.

"That seems to cover it," I say and then I turn and head down the corridor.

It's just past four o'clock when I step back onto Sixth Avenue. Rush hour is underway. The flight to the suburbs and to weekend retreats has begun and traffic is starting to to snarl. I don't believe Harvey Junior. He's too slick, his answers too pat. Maybe it comes with the profession. Realtors, like used car salesmen, seem to be born with a mangled moral compass. Harvey is no better or worse than the rest of them but I wouldn't trust him even if he told me that snowballs were cold.

I look around for a cab and that's when I see him. Or rather I should say, I see THEM. Biff is just emerging from a coffee shop across the street in the company of a tall thin balding man with a prominent long needle-like nose. His eyebrows are bushy and his eyes are set close together. They chat for a moment and then walk off in different directions. Biff has his hands jammed into his trouser pockets and he doesn't look happy. At that moment my view of him is obscured by a city bus which is passing by a foot or two at a time, stopping and starting as horns blare from every direction. As the bus goes by I see myself staring once again at the face of my old commanding officer, Captain John Crosby, and I remember that we have a dinner date, I also remember that I am due at the production office to show the flag and watch some film. For the briefest of moments I think about calling Harold Hecht and asking if John could tag along but no, I know the answer without asking. Critics gets to see the finished product and nothing less. It's an immutable law of the profession. The bus picks up speed. I look across the street. Biff has disappeared.

I look around for a handy phone booth. Dinner with John will have to wait.

CHAPTER ELEVEN

The Cameron Hotel is located in the Bronx on Gun Hill Road near Rte. One. It's old and seedy but it's three stories high and plenty big enough to handle the needs of a motion picture company operating on a shoestring budget. I've taken a cab because, although I have a perfectly good rental car stashed in the Astor garage, I have no stomach for dealing with the pre-weekend traffic which has swelled to gargantuan proportions. I exit the cab and am paying the driver, tipping him handsomely, when Gene Kelly hurries out of the front entrance. He looks in my direction and waves. I think he's waving at me so I wave back, but no, he's waving at the cabbie. He jogs toward us.

"Hi," he says to me with a half-hearted smile.

"Hi," I say back as he hops into the back seat of the cab. "Waldorf-Astoria," he says. The cabbie flips the flag and off they go. This is when I remember that Kelly is married to Betsy Blair who is Borgnine's co-star. Silly me. For a moment, I thought he'd just been slumming.

Inside I check at the desk for the location of the production office. The clerk points to the end of the hallway where I will find elevators and a stairway to the lower floor. I take the stairs. A man must exercise when he gets the chance.

The Black Watch Salon is a large meeting room which has been converted into the production office, the nerve center for any film company on location. It looks like every other production office I've ever seen, maybe a little sparser. A few tables, a few chairs, a mimeo machine, several typewriters, a coffee maker and a water cooler, phones everywhere, a large standing blackboard with indecipherable notes scratched all over it. I feel right at home. A geeky looking guy who looks like a college kid is at one of the desks typing and a young girl is collating some material at a long table. I see no sign of Ruby so she's probably still at the location. The only other person in the room is Betsy Blair who is sitting off in a corner leafing through some pink colored pages. These are script changes for tomorrow's work.

I walk over to her.

"Miss Blair?"

She looks up.

"Hi," she says.

"I'm Joe Bernardi. Bowles & Bernardi. We're doing publicity for the picture."

She throws me a wry expression which almost passes for a smile. "So nice to hear it. We thought you'd gone back to the coast without saying goodbye."

"I deserve that, " I say. She's no beauty like Taylor or Gardner but she's got an attractive face, twinkly eyes and a shapely body. In the script, her character, Clara the schoolteacher, is described as a dog. If she's a dog, then I'm Rin Tin Tin. Maybe they're planning to fit her with buck teeth and a few well placed facial warts. I hope not.

"Forgive me," I say. "I've been remiss for which I apologize. Won't happen again. By the way, I ran into your husband outside. He stole my cab."

"Oh, I'm so sorry," she says.

"It's all right. I was through with it."

She smiles. This time it's real. "Well, if he seemed a little distracted, he's in town doing press rounds for Brigadoon and it's not going all that well."

The movie version of the Lerner & Loewe musical opened five days ago to decent business and mixed reviews.

"Did you catch Bosley Crowther in the Times this morning?" she asks. Afraid not, I tell her. "A solid pan, top to bottom. Gene's furious. They were supposed to shoot in Scotland, then the bean counters at MGM made him pull it back to the soundstages on the backlot. Not the movie he wanted to make."

I shake my head sympathetically.

"And not the best way to treat the most valuable talent you have under contract," I say.

"Maybe not for much longer."

"Oh?"

"Gene's dying to do 'Guys and Dolls' for Goldwyn but the studio won't loan him out."

"Strike two," I say.

She nods. "He owes them two more pictures and I think that'll be it."

I shake my head tenuously.

"I wonder, Miss Blair, I mean,do you really think you should be telling me all this?"

She breaks out in laughter.

"No problem, Mr. Bernardi. Gene's telling everybody in town including Winchell and Ed Sullivan. And please call me Betsy."

"Only if you call me Joe. What's a good time to get together for a Q and A and some photographs?"

"Gene's flying back to the coast Sunday. How about Monday? I'm free all day."

"Monday's fine," I say. "I'll set it up."

Betsy looks past me toward the entrance as we both hear voices approaching. The crew starts to filter in led by Ruby. Several of them go directly to the table with the pink pages. A couple head for the coffee brewer amidst a lot of good natured banter. Toby Krantz and Paddy Chayefsky are standing in the doorway in deep conversation with the director of photography Joe LaShelle. Some pictures have happy sets, some don't. This one seems to be happier than most.

Ruby spots me and waves. I wave back. She points to her wrist watch. I check mine. Ten minutes to six. I nod in understanding.

Fifteen minutes later I am sitting on a folding chair in a small conference room down the hall from the production office. A screen has been placed at one end of the room and a couple of dozen chairs have been set up for viewing the dailies. The film editor will be operating the projector. I'm sitting between Chayefsky and Harold Hecht. Delbert Mann, the director, is directly in front of me. Ernie Borgnine is off to the side sitting with Joe Mantell who plays Marty's best friend, Angie. Mantell is one of several cast members who had appeared in the original television version. The room is jammed because anyone who wants to see the dailies is welcome to sit in. Several crew members have found places on the floor as the lights dim and the projector starts up.

It doesn't take me long to realize I am watching something very special. Ernie and Betsy are sitting in a diner across from one another chatting. It isn't what they say that's so important as the way they say it. Ernie is alternately warm and outgoing and then awkward, a little afraid of saying the wrong thing, comfortable with this woman he has just met, able to talk to her easily for maybe the frst time in his life. And Betsy plays off of him brilliantly, shy and quiet, then smiling and even laughing, letting down her defenses, opening up to this suddenly garrulous friendly man she has known less than two hours.

The lights come up thirty minutes later. I've watched the scene play out from every angle and I was never bored. The crew is bubbling with enthusiasm as they file out. I continue to stare at the blank screen until I realize that Harold is talkng to me.

"Well?" he says.

I turn to him.

"Is there someplace you and I can talk privately?" I ask.

A slight frown passes across his face but he says sure, not a problem. He leads me out of the room and down the hall into a small unused meeting room. He flips on the lights and shuts the door, then turns to me.

"Okay, what is it?"

"I can't do this," I say. "You need to get someone else."

His eyes narrow in annoyance. "Is that right? I think we have a pretty good little picture on our hands," he says.

At that moment the door opens and Chayefsky and Mann enter.

"What's the problem?" Chayefsky asks.

"Mr. Bernardi was just telling me he can't handle the picture for us. He suggested we retain someone else."

Chayefsky gives me a hard look.

I shake my head.

"You have me all wrong. I love what I've seen. It's brilliant. You have every reason to be proud but I'm sorry, I can't do you justice. Something is going on in my life that needs my full attention and I won't— I can't— work on this picture if I can't give you my best effort."

"Tell me," Harold says.

"It's complicated," I say.

"Tell me anyway. I'm not going anywhere."

And so I do. I tell them about my long and fruitless search for Bunny and then having found her, the trauma she suffered watching her friend be killed in a jail cell and that only a jammed gun barrel saved her from a similar fate. I tell them about stashing her someplace where she won't be found and laying a futile trap for the killer.

"He knows she can identify him. He knows he has to kill her to keep her quiet and I have to do everything I can to make sure he doesn't. I'm going to need every ounce of my strength, every minute of the day to go after this guy and I am not going to cheat you and this picture by going through the motions. I hope you understand."

"You're cooperating with the police?" Delbert Mann asks.

"Yes."

Mann looks at Chayefsky who looks at Hecht and then they all look at each other. Hecht finally looks at me.

"We'll wait," he says.

"Oh, no, I couldn't ask—"

"We'll wait, Joe," he repeats firmly. "You're the best and we want you. Another week or two isn't going to make a difference. If after that this guy is still on the loose, we'll talk again. In the meantime, do what you have to do."

I look from Hecht to the other two. They both nod. I feel myself tearing up. I put out my hand. All three reach in and we jointly grasp each others hands. Suddenly I hope this ambitious little picture makes a hundred mlllion dollars.

By eight o'clock I'm in a cab on the way back to the Astor and mulling my next move. Bunny is safe but I realize I am not, not unless I switch hotel rooms. Daphne's killer may have skipped last night but there's nothing to stop him from trying tonight and I'm in no shape for another all night vigil even if I could talk Horvath into it and even if I wanted to which I don't.

The first sign of trouble comes when we turn onto Broadway from West 44th Street and a uniformed cop looms up in front of our cab, waving us toward a detour. My driver rolls down his window and asks what's going on. The cop brusquely tells him to keep moving. By this time I have spotted the police barricades by the front entrance of the hotel and the three squad cars parked at curbside, red and white lights flashing as the cops try to keep the rubber neckers away. An ambulance with its rear doors open is backed up to the front door.

I reach in my wallet and take out a twenty which I hand to the driver telling him I'll walk the rest of the way. I hurry along the sidewalk, shoving my way through the crowd craning for a closer look at the police activity. Near the entrance a uniform tries to block my way but I show him my room key and he lets me pass. I still have no idea what's going on but something tells me I'm involved. It turns out I'm right.

I spot Horvath immediately. He's standing near the elevators in deep conversation with two uniforms and a guy in civvies. Horvath sees me and waves me over. As I stride toward him the elevator doors open and the ambulance driver and a medic emerge wheeling a gurney toward the front door. A uniform is running interference and moving people out of the way. As the gurney passes by I look down at Vicki Caputo. She's hooked up to an IV and there is a puffy blood stained bandage swathed around her neck. Her face is the color of blackboard chalk.

I turn as Horvath and the guy in civvies reach me.

"What happened?" I ask.

"The son of a bitch finally made his move," Horvath says. "Al Feeney, Joe Bernardi."

I nod at the guy in civvies. He's a beefy guy with a round florid face. His jacket's off and I can see he sweats a lot. I can also see that he's shaken up. Whoever says that cops get used to things like this has it all wrong.

"Six o'clock came and Vicki called my room," Feeney says, his voice cracking slightly. "She said she wanted to give it a couple more hours so I said sure, what the hell. Comes eight o'clock and there's still no sign of the guy so she calls me again and says she's had enough. I agree. Day wasted, I think. I get my things and open the door and when I step out into the hallway, Vicki's just coming out of her room. She's got the outfit on, you know the scarf and the dark glasses and right away I see this waiter across the way standing next to this food cart. Before I can say anything he whips out his gun and he fires at her, point blank, catches her right here—" He indicates his throat. "She goes down and I take out my piece and I fire two shots at the guy. One hits him because I spun him around but he raises his gun at me and as he fires I duck back into the doorway to my room. I wait for a second, then look and the guy is tear-assing down the hallway toward the stairway. I fire off one more shot but miss. That's when I look down at Vicki and she's losing blood all over the place. I grab that scarf and I try to stem the blood flow just as a guy across the hall peers out of his doorway. I tell him to call an ambulance and the police and for the next fifteen minutes I'm trying to keep the kid from bleeding to death."

"How bad?" I ask Horvath.

"Bad enough," he says, "but the medic says she has a chance."

I look at Feeney.

"The shooter, He matched the sketch?"

"Close enough."

"And you're sure you hit him?"

"Al hit him, Joe," Horvath says. "There was a blood trail all over the staircase leading down. We've alerted the hospitals and the city doctors know the drill. If he goes for medical help, we'll get him."

I nod.

"Where'd they take Vicki?" I ask.

"Bellevue," Horvath says.

I nod and start across the lobby. Horvath calls after me.

"Joe, it'll be hours before they know anything. There's nothing you can do for her. You need sleep."

"I'll sleep tomorrow," I say continuing on to the main entrance. Whatever happens with Vicki, I'm going to be there. No time is a good time to be raced to a hospital for treatment but Fridays are worse than most. The waiting room is a cauldron of whining, crying and screaming humanity. The cops are on hand with their gunshot victims, sometimes the perpetrator, sometimes the prey. Terrified parents have brought in their kid who tumbled down a staircase. They wait anxiously for news, sitting next to a hooker whose best friend has o.d.'ed on skag or horse or any of a dozen drugs designed to put you out of your mind and into a lethal coma. A three car pile up just outside the Queens Midtown Tunnel has supplied four more victims one of whom was wheeled in minus an arm. A Puerto Rican kid named Spik who got into a knife fight with an Italian kid named Dago is lying on a gurney with two punctures in his abdomen. I heard a nurse tell another nurse that he probably won't make it. If he doesn't he dies alone. There isn't a parent in sight.

From nine until almost midnight a parade of cops shows up, asking at the desk about Vicki. They're told what I was told. Nothing. Some stay for a while, others leave vowing to call later. A little after ten a short heavy set woman with grey streaked black hair arrives accompanied by a thin balding man with a droopy mustache. I find out later this is Vicki's mother and her uncle. Her makeup is mussed, her eyes red from crying. She takes a seat across the room and stares stoically straight ahead. The uncle brings her coffee. She hardly notices. As the time passes the room becomes more crowded, the noise more unbearable.

Twice I get up and go outside to drink in the cool night air and maybe expunge the sight of Vicki on the gurney from my memory. I don't kid myself. I know how easily that could have been Bunny lying there, bleeding profusely, her skin as pale as alabaster. The thought of it makes me shudder. I think about the shooter, scurrying around the city like a rat in a maze, bleeding from his wound, and desperately seeking help where there is none. I pray he is caught soon. Even more fervently I pray he doesn't bleed to death before he tells us the name of the person who hired him.

A few minutes past eleven Horvath shows up having secured the crime scene and left Feeney in charge. He's booked me into a room on another floor and hands me the key. He tells me to go. I tell him I'll stay. When I ask he says there's no word yet on the shooter. An APB has been issued to all squad cars. Two man details armed with the police artist's sketches have been sent to Grand Central and Penn Stations as well as the Port Authority Bus Terminal. Every cop in town wants a piece of this bastard and so do I.

Finally, at quarter past one, a doctor appears looking for someone from the police department. Horvath talks to him. There's a lot of nodding of heads and then the doctor goes back into the bowels of the hospital. Horvath pulls me aside and tells me Vicki's in good shape. They went in and got the bullet, sewed her up and shot her full of antibiotics and painkillers. At the moment she's resting comfortably with an IV drip to help her sleep. No visitors, not tonight. Again Horvath tells me to leave. This time he doesn't have to tell me twice. By the time I get back to the Astor I'm wiped out,. I find my new room in the sixth floor and let myself in. All my belongings are there, transfered from the room upstairs. I kick off my shoes and flop down on the bed. For a few moments I catch myself staring at the ceiling and then exhaustion envelops me and my eyelids droop and then I remember nothing more.

CHAPTER TWELVE

I sit bolt upright in bed. Something has awakened me and I suspect it's my subconscious telling me that I have places to go and people to see and no time for lollygagging around in bed. The clock on the nightstand reads 9:02. I pick up the phone and put in a call to Sergeant Horvath. He's not in yet but the guy on the phone knows who I am and he gives me a rundown. Vicki Caputo is awake and responsive and being fed intravenously. It'll be a while before she'll be able to swallow solid food. There's no sign of the shooter. He's either dead or out there bleeding to death. Either way is okay with the boys in the squad room. After I hang up I pad my way into the bathroom to brush my teeth. There is one thing I believe, that somewhere out there in this teeming city is Daphne's killer, wounded and bleeding while the cops scour every street and back alley searching for him. Somebody may know where he's hiding and it's my best guess that that somebody is Harvey Claymore Junior.

It takes me seven minutes to dress and one more minute to find the yellow pages in the bottom drawer of the nightstand. I make a call out.

"Claymore Properties. How may I help you?" The voice is female and throaty and a little come hither. I wonder if her legs are anything like her voice. Even though it's Saturday I knew they'd be open for business. Real estate people never sleep.

"Harvey Claymore, please," I say.

"Junior or senior?"

"Junior," I say.

"I'm sorry, Mr. Claymore Junior is not in. May I take a message?"

Then I remember he is flying off to Atlantic City this morning. Or at least he was supposed to. I wonder if last night's events changed his plans.

"I was supposed to meet him later this afternoon at a hotel in Atlantic City and I've lost the name of it."

"I wouldn't know anything about that, sir."

"Perhaps there's a notation on his appointments calendar."

"I'm sorry, sir. Is there someone else that can help you?"

The not-so-suibtle brushoff. I hesitate for a second, remembering what Junior said about his father having Daphne followed.

"Harvey Senior. Is he in?"

"May I tell him who's calling?"

No, you may not, I think to myself as I hang up. I have a few questions for the old man which are better asked face to face. No sense warning him I'm on the prowl.

Claymore Properties has offices on the third floor of an older office building on Eighth Avenue and 41st Street. I walk it. It's not the kind of place you'd find IBM or Mobil Oil but I suspect that old man Claymore is more into cheap rent and less into ostentation. The elevator creaks and groans but it gets there and a few moments later I am standing at the reception desk.

"May I help you, sir?" It's that same syrup-laden voice I heard over the phone. I should be excited but in this case my imagination has trumped reality. She's 50 if she's a day, short but buxom with salt-and-pepper hair and thick glasses with ruby red frames hanging from a chain around her neck. She stares at me through thickly mascaraed eyelashes. I deftly hide my disappointment.

"Mr. Claymore, Senior," I say.

"Do you have an appointment, sir?"

"No, but he'll see me." I give her my name and she picks up the phone and buzzes through to the old man's inner sanctum. After a moment she replaces the receiver.

"He suggests you call for an appointment," she says icily.

"I suggest he gives me five minutes so I can tell him which city his son flew into this morning to buy a broken down hotel you couldn't give away to a family of squatters."

Somewhat unwillingly, she relays the message, perhaps not in those exact words and a couple of minutes later I find myself being ushered into Harvey Claymore Senior's serviceable but far from luxurious office. He's standing at a window looking down at the street below.

Without preamble and without even looking at me, he asks, "What's all this about a hotel?"

When pressed I can be as rude as the next guy so I pull up a chair by his desk and say, "I could use a coffee. One cream, one sugar, and if you've got a cookie or two, that would be nice. I missed breakfast just to be here with you."

Claymore walks over to the desk and stares down at me. I smile politely. He picks up the phone and places my order and than sits down, eyeing me like I was a cockroach wading around in his oatmeal. The other day in the dim light of the Carnegie Deli he didn't look all that well. This morning he looks cadaverous. Junior is right. Senior has already started on that long slide into oblivion.

"The other day at lunch I thought you and I had reached an accommodation," Claymore says to me. "Your dismissal of Anselm Forsythe told me otherwise. I find you annoying, Mr. Bernardi. Annoying and far too inquisitive."

"I'm happy to see you're paying attention. Tell me about the man you hired to follow Daphne Gennaro."

"I don't know what you're talking about."

I reach in my jacket pocket and take out the police sketch. I unfold it and hold it up for him to see. He glares at me.

"I've seen that picture and I've told the police, I have no idea who that man is."

"Harvey Junior says differently."

"My son believes in flying saucers."

At that moment the buxom babe from the front desk enters with my coffee and a stale-looking donut. I thank her. She forgets to smile. After she leaves I dunk my donut and turn my attention back to Harvey Senior.

"Did you not tell him you would disinherit him if he didn't get rid of the woman?"

"I did, but I didn't have to have either one of them followed to be assured that my wishes would be respected. My son is an adroit realtor but a spineless human being. He would not defy me."

"Nice to have such certainty," I say with a half smile.

He starts to say something and then suddenly goes into a coughing spasm. The blood drains from his face as he reaches in his pocket for that vial of tiny pills.

"Water," he croaks pointing to a sideboard where I see a pitcher and a glass. I get up quickly and pour water into the glass and give it to him. He takes two swallows and the coughing abates. Meanwhile he's gotten a pill out of the vial and he places it under his tongue. He sits perfectly still, holding his breath as it dissolves. After what seems like eons he slowly exhales and a faint blush of color returns to his face.

"Will you be all right?" I ask.

"Yes, thank you," he nods. "Just give me a moment." He has a death grip on the arms of his chair and he seems almost afraid to move. Then slowly he starts to relax and settle back. Carefully, he slips the vial back into his shirt pocket and looks over at me.

"Since you are suggesting that I had that woman followed, you are also implying that I hired that person to kill her." Claymore says.

"The thought crossed my mind. And you need to see a doctor."

He shakes his head in disgust.

"The idea that I would order or sanction murder is ludicrous. Assuming for a moment that this woman was pregnant and carrying my son's child, the problem could have easily been resolved with money. Certainly more money than she'd ever seen in her lifetime. And if for some bizarre reason she chose to continue her quest for marriage and a piece of the Claymore fortune, the matter could always be adjudicated in the courts. I have an eight figure net worth, sir, and I can afford very bright, very expensive attorneys. She would be lucky to find a lawyer of any skill level who would be willing to take me on. Murder? No, no, Mr. Bernardi. The idea is absurd."

I start to do the math on my fingers.

"Eight figures. That would mean—"

"Yes, it would," Claymore says flatly.

"And yet, the woman is dead, murdered in a jail cell and I have to wonder how and why."

"I don't," Claymore says. "She is no longer any of my business. As I said to you at lunch, look to her past. A former client, a jilted lover, some deranged pervert from years ago. There is where your focus should lie." He smiles."Now, about that out of town hotel."

I'm ready to tell him but at that moment, I hear loud voices coming from outside the office. Claymore hears them too. One of them belongs to the receptionist. The other to a man and I think I recognize it. 'You can't go in there', 'Get of my way', 'There's someone in there. I have my orders', 'Screw your orders, lady'!

The door flies open and a young man bursts into the room. I've seen him once before, yesterday at the building on Sixth Avenue. The receptionist is right behind him and is in a high state of agitation.

"I'm sorry, Mr Claymore, I couldn't stop him."

"It's all right, Velma. What are you doing here, Biff? You know my wishes."

"To hell with your wishes, Pop," Biff Claymore says. He is acting like a man possessed and when he looks in my direction, his demeanor gets worse.

"You! What are you doing here? Who the hell are you?" he says stepping toward me angrily. I get up out of the chair and back away. He looks mad enough to kill.

"Take it easy, fella. Just back off," I say, still easing away from him.

At that moment Abe Fallon lumbers into the room and grabs Biff by the back of his jacket, yanking him backwards.

"You know the rules, Biff. You're not wanted around here. Now don't make trouble. Let's go."

Biff tries to wriggle loose as he looks frantically toward his father.

"He's dead, Pop!" he gasps.

"Who's dead?"

"Harvey! He killed himself!"

"What?"

Harvey Senior turns white, his face contorted into an expression of disbelief.

"Over at the Sixth Avenue property. He opened one of the windows and jumped. Eleven stories! My God, Pop!" He shrugs off Fallon and goes to his father, tears running down his cheeks, hands on the desk and leaning forward. "I'm so sorry, Pop. I can't believe it. My God, it's awful."

The old man looks at him with hollow haunted eyes. "Are you sure, Biff? No mistake? It couldn't have been someone else?"

"No, the cops wouldn't let me in but Gallagher, the security guy, he's the one who found him while he was making rounds. There was a note on the desk. It said 'I'm sorry'. That's all. Just 'I'm sorry.'

Then Gallagher saw the open window and when he went over and looked down, there he was, Pop, laying there on the pavement, all crumpled up like a rag doll." He whirls around in my direction, shoving a finger toward me. "Him! He was there yesterday with Harv! "

"I didn't harm your brother," I say.

"And who the hell are you?"

I tell him. "And yesterday when I left him, your brother was alive and well and looking forward to flying down to Atlantic City this morning to make an offer on a hotel."

"You're a liar!"

"I don't think so," I reply.

Suddenly Biff leaps forward trying to grab me by the throat, He's younger than me by maybe nine or ten years but he's short and scrawny and I'm able to throw him aside. He hits the floor hard and rolls over.

Claymore gets to his feet angrily.

"Stop this at once!" he shouts.

Biff gets to his feet and pulls out a knife, what the city gang members call a pigsticker. He comes at me with a manic look on his face and now I'm the one backing up.

"Biff! Put that away! Abe!" Claymore shouts.

Fallon pushes past me, shoving me to one side as he confronts Biff.

"Stay out of this, Abe," Biff whines.

"Put it down, Biff. Now. Drop it on the floor," Fallon tells him.

Biff shakes his head violently, holding the knife out in front of him. Fallon takes a step toward him, feints left and when Biff reacts Fallon grabs his knife hand by the wrist and twists it violently. Biff screams in pain as the knife clatters to the floor and he is spun around, Fallon's arm around his throat and his arm yanked up behind his back.

"Abe! That's enough!" Claymore says.

The big man releases his grip and pushes Biff away, then bends down to retrieve the knife from the floor. Biff is on his knees weeping openly. I stare at him and then look over to Harvey Senior who meets my gaze.

"Maybe you'd better leave, Mr. Bernardi," he says quietly. I agree. My business here is done with. I need to find Sergeant Horvath and get some answers.

Outside I grab a cab and on a hunch go across town to the Sixth Avenue high-rise office building. I'm not surprised to find the place crawling with cops. It's a daylight version of the scene last evening at the the Astor. I make it as far as the front entrance before I'm stopped by a uniform in charge of crowd control. I tell him I'm working the case with Horvath which he doesn't believe but I finally get him to radio Horvath who is overseeing the crime scene up on the eleventh floor. Horvath tells him to send me up.

When I step off the elevator I'm confronted with a swarm of activity. A couple of print guys are dusting in every logical place they can think of though there aren't that many. I see two photographers and several other techs who are gathering up dirt and dust samples for lab analysis. I also spot Horvath down at the end of the corridor talking with a white haired little man in a Burberry raincoat and an Irish cap. When I reach them, Horvath introduces me. His name is Horace Hatfield and he is a doctor and he says he considers himself lucky to be alive.

"Tell Mr. Bernardi what you told me, Doctor," Horvath says.

"It was dreadful, sir. Exceedingly dreadful," Hatfield says. "It was just after ten. I was exhausted after a long day at the hospital and I was getting ready to turn in when there was a knock on my door. Very unusual. Very unexpected. But I thought perhaps it was a tenant in the building who needed some minor patchup. I do that for them. I'm a good neighbor. But as soon as I started to open the door, these two men forced their way in."

"Two men?" I ask, puzzled.

"Yes. One man was badly injured, I saw that right away. The other was holding a gun."

"The wounded guy was our shooter. Doctor Hatfield confirmed it from our sketch," Horvath says.

"And the other man?" I say.

"I really couldn't tell you what he looks like," Hatfield says. "He wore dark glasses, a baseball cap pulled down over his forehead and a blue windbreaker zipped up to his chin. Anyway they tell me to fix up the man who was wounded and if I do, I won't get hurt."

"Anyone else in the house with you? A wife?" I ask.

One of the tech guys comes over and pulls Horvath aside and begins to talk to him quietly.

"No, I'm a widower," Hatfield says. "It was just me. Anyway I have a small treatment room in the back and I got him up on the table. He was suffering from a nasty gunshot wound in his side that was starting to get infected. I checked for an exit wound but there was none which meant the bullet was still lodged inside him. I must have worked on him for an hour but I got the bullet, cleaned out the wound, shot him full of penicillin and painkillers, and taped him up. I told him he needed at least two or three days of rest but he just laughed at me. They tied me to the table, grabbed some antibiotics and painkillers and bandages and left. I struggled for a long time but it was no use. Those good old boys know how to tie their knots."

"Good old boys?" I say alertly.

"Southerners. Deep south like the Carolinas or Georgia. Can't be more specific. They all sound pretty much the same to me."

I nod.

"Let's say this fella doesn't rest up. What happens to him?"

Hatfield shrugs.

"His system's run down. He lost a lot of blood. He could just keel over. Or maybe not. There's no way to predict."

"Okay," I say. "Now this other man, the one with the gun. You say you can't identify him."

"Not a chance."

"Tall? Short?"

"Medium height maybe."

"Tell me about his baseball cap. What team was it?" I ask.

"No team," Hatfield says. "It was a cap like the ones ballplayers wear but it had a logo. Pennzoil, I think."

"And what about his jacket?"

"What about it?"

"Any markings? Patches? Logos?"

Hatfield frowns, trying to remember. Then he nods.

"The sleeve. Down one of the sleeves it read 'Valvoline'."

At that moment Horvath rejoins us. He looks at me.

"Well, what do you think?" he asks.

"I see racing cars. I see a place in Connecticut called Lime Rock and most of all I see Biff Claymore."

"Excuse me, Sergeant," Hatfield interrupts, "but I'm due at the hospital in a few minutes. If there's nothing else—"

"No, nothing," Horvath says, "and thanks for coming by, Doctor. We'll probably need a signed statement but it can wait. We'll be in touch."

"Right," Hatfield says, tipping his hat and then walking off. Horvath looks back at me.

"What's all this about Biff Claymore?" he asks.

"According to his father he's up to his eyeballs in business with a bunch of car nuts trying to build a racetrack in the northwest corner of Connecticut."

"So he needs a few dollars for an investment. How does that add up to murdering Daphne Gennaro?"

"I don't know," I say, "but four hundred and fifty thousand dollars is more than just a few bucks."

"You sure about that number?"

"Heard it with my own ears." I look at my watch. "Twenty minutes to twelve. I think I'm going to take a ride up there."

"What for?" Horvath asks.

"Look around. Ask a few questions."

"To what end, Joe?"

"I'm not sure but I know if you start poking a stick into a gopher hole, pretty soon the gopher pops his head out to see what's going on."

"Oh, great," Horvath says in exasperation. "We may be dealing with a stone cold killer here and you want to go poking at him with a stick. Are you out of your mind?"

"Somebody has to check it out. If not me, who?"

"Not me," Horvath says. "I have no jurisdiction."

"My point exactly," I say.

"God damn it, Bernardi, you are not a cop and you are not equipped to go up against this s.o.b. whoever he is."

"I'm not planning to get into a gunfight with the guy. But maybe you'd like to join me, Unofficially, of course." He shakes his head "I've got a case to wrap up here," he says.

"Well, while you're wrapping, be very careful how you throw around that word 'suicide'."

"We've got a note."

"You've got two words of block printing that say 'I'm sorry" and from what I hear they could have been written by a five-year old. By me that's not a suicide note. Not even close. I was with this guy yesterday, Sarge. He was looking forward to flying into Atlantic City and screwing some poor bastard out of his hotel for a pocketful of dimes and nickels. His eyes were lit up like Christmas ornaments and he was no more suicidal than an Irish sweepstakes winner."

"I don't suppose you can prove that," Horvath says.

"My theory's just as good as yours," I say. "Besides my number one problem is the guy in the sketch and until I see him laid out in the county morgue, toes up, I'm going to keep digging no matter where it takes me. My lady, your witness, is not going to spend the rest of her life staring over her shoulder."

I start to walk back toward the elevators. Horvath calls after me. "You get in trouble up there, you're on your own," he warns.

I toss him a wry smile. "The story of my life, Sarge." I head toward the elevators again and I don't look back.

CHAPTER THIRTEEN

By one o'clock I'm on the Merritt Parkway leaving New York. I turn north at the intersection with Rt. 7. Lakeville, home base for the race course, is about two hours away. I don't know exactly what I'm looking for or what I expect to find. Maybe I'm taking a Pennzoil cap, a Valvoline jacket, and thick Southern accents and making a wild leap of illogic. If so all I'm wasting is time. But I do know this. I can't sit around New York City, clueless and waiting for something to happen. I wasn't kidding about the stick and the gopher hole. I want this murderous son of a bitch to know I'm coming after him.

At one-thirty I stop in Danbury for gas and a quick sandwich and coffee and after that, it's north again on 7, paralleling the famous Appalachian Trail through some spectacular scenic wilderness areas. As I'd surmised, traffic is light and I'm making excellent time except for a ten minute jam up in New Milford. By the time I reach Lime Rock Road, the turnoff for Lakeville, my watch reads 3:15. Almost immediately after I make the turn I see a huge sign that's been erected by the side of the road off to my right. "Future Home of the Lime Rock Race Course" and below that in smaller letters, "Terranova Construction". Next to the sign is a dirt road which leads into the trees. I take it and after about five hundred yards I emerge into a clearing. Off to my left is a security shack. In front of me are three huge bulldozers sitting quiet and unmanned. Beyond them I can see that a considerable section of the property has been cleared of trees and leveled.

I get out of my car to take a closer look. As I'm walking toward the bulldozers, the door to the security shack opens and a burly guy in a light grey uniform steps out. He carries a holstered pistol on his hip.

"Afternoon," he calls out affably, walking toward me.

"Hi," I say. The patch on his sleeve reads "Wainwright Protection Services". Stitched over his shirt pocket is the name 'Ervin'. The guy is hired help, strictly unofficial.

"Can I help you with something, sir?" he asks.

"Just looking," I say. "A buddy of mine back in New York told me about this place. Helluva a good idea. Get the race cars off the road and onto a track where they belong."

"That's the plan." Ervin says.

I look around.

"Where is everybody? You're not shut down, I hope."

"It's Saturday, sir. They knocked off at noon. You'll find everybody in Lakeville. most likely hanging around the hotel or Faraday's Chop Shop."

"Doesn't seem like they've made a lot of progress," I say. "How long ago did they break ground?"

"Maybe two weeks ago. Why do you ask, sir?"

"Oh, I don't know. Just curious. I heard money was tight."

A little flicker of caution shows in the guard's eyes.

"And where'd you hear that, sir?

"From my buddy." I hesitate. "Look, I'll level wirh you. The guy's not exactly a buddy. We met at some dive in Little Italy last week and we got to drinking and he was telling me how there was a potload of money to be made in this place if I got in right away.

I've got a few bucks to invest so here I am. I'l tell you something funny. I was so pickled I can't even remember the guy's name. Wait a second." I reach in my pocket and take out the rumpled artist's sketch of Daphne's killer and show it to the guy. "This is him. I keep wanting to say Andy or Alan but that's not right. Can you help me out with this?"

The guard takes the sketch and makes an elaborate show of studying it.

"Could be a lot of people," he says thoughtfully. No, it couldn't, I think to myself, but I humor him by agreeing. He hands it back. "Sorry, can't help you."

I shrug.

"Doesn't matter. Guess I'll drive over to Lakeville and look around. Nice idea, this place. Could really be something. Well, thanks for the tour. Be seein' you."

I get back in my car and start to turn around as the rent-a-cop goes back into the shack, leaving the door open. As I start out toward Rt. 7, I look in my rear view mirror and see that Ervin is talking to someone on the phone. I wonder if Lakeville is planning to roll out the red carpet for me.

The answer is no. Right after I pass Mononskopomuc Lake I find a sign which reads "Lakeville Welcomes You - Population 1879" and turn onto Montgomery Street which, according to my map, leads to the center of town. No one from Welcome Wagon pops out of the shrubbery. A marching band is nowhere to be seen. The only living soul in sight is an old man pushing a wheelbarrow. He is not the Mayor and he does not hand me the key to the city. In fact he doesn't seem to notice me at all. Five hundred yards further along, civilization begins to show itself. Small houses to the left and right sit on well-tended half-acre lots. I continue onto Main Street. Both sides of the thoroughfare are lined with storefronts, all neatly kept up and apparently thriving. Most of the parking spots are taken and the sidewalks are jammed with shoppers, Saturday afternoon in small town America. I could just as easily have been in Murfreesboro, Tennessee, or East McKeesport, Pennsylvania. I feel right at home.

I glance down a side street and get a quick glimpse of the Monarch Hotel. It's three stories high and substantial looking and I think when locals refer to "the" hotel, this is the one they're talking about. Ahead on my right at the end of the block I see the sign for Faraday's Chop Shop. Next to it is a parking lot which is pretty much full. I suspect that the Lime Rock crowd has taken over the place. I get lucky. I find a parking spot between a chopped down Model A with oversized tires and a Chevy truck with a Confederate flag painted on the tailgate and a gun rack in the cab. As I walk toward the front entrance I'm struck by the overwhelming number of license tags from Virginia and Kentucky and points south. If the Civil War is suddenly rekindled in this laconic little town, I fear for the indigenous Yankee population.

I walk through the door and I'm struck by three things. The crowd, the noise and the body odor. The shouting and the laughter are drowning out the adenoidal singer on the jukebox who is lamenting "If You Ain't Lovin', You Ain't Livin'." A tiny dance floor is jammed with guys in work shirts and cowboy hats dancing with gals in scoop necked dresses that stop just above the knees. Each time one them twirls around, it raises a lot of hooting and hollering from several nearby tables crowded with fun-loving drunks. The scene reminds me a lot of my days working the oil fields of Oklahoma which is unfortunate because those are days I'd just as soon forget.

I find myself a spot at the end of the bar and order a Schlitz in the bottle. Then I turn my attention to the faces in the room. I'm looking for dark hair. I see a whole lot of baseball caps. I look for dark sideburns. I see a lot of those too. This may be tougher than

I thought. Absentmindedly I pick up a menu. It says "Chops and steaks. If you can name it, we can prepare it. Barbecue Every Night. All you can eat $9.95." I find myself wondering how a place like this ended up in the heart of Yankeedom and immediately I know the answer. The people behind Lime Rock are dead serious and commitment to the project means commitment to the people who work for them. Crab cakes and scrod just aren't going to cut it with good old boys from Dixie.

"Howdy."

A voice at my elbow. I turn. Lean and lanky and maybe an inch shorter than me, he's ruddy-faced and redheaded and one of the few patrons without a cap. His windbreaker carries the logo for Team Luckett over his heart. Across from it is his name, Rance.

"You must be the fella stopped by the construction site," he says.

"Guess you must have heard from Ervin," I say.

"Rance Luckett," he says, putting out his hand.

"Charlie Berger," I say, appropriating my former boss's name as we shake. Charlie won't mind and I don't risk forgetting a phony name I just invented. The bartender brings me my bottle of beer and I down a healthy swallow. The guy with the adenoids has given way to some babe telling some guy "There's Poison in Your Heart". These country singers sure know how to wallow in misery.

"The work site's not much to look at now, Charlie," Rance is saying, "but it will be. You a racing fan?"

"Used to be right after the war. Kinda lost track. You boys from the South are turning all that horsepower into something special."

"Hell, man, we're sure trying. So how'd you hear about us?"

"Guy I met in a bar in New York City. He told me this place was going to be a money machine. That's my business. Sinking money into money machines."

"This fella in the bar. He have a name?"

"Not one I can remember," I say. "We were pretty sloshed. I

remember he had dark sideburns down to his jawline and his hair was jet black and kinda greasy. Sorta like the fellas here in the bar. Why? Is there a problem?"

"No, not really," Luckett says. "We'd like to keep everything a little quiet is all. Some of the folks around here ain't all that keen on us being here. We're trying to mind our own business and be good neighbors"

"Gotcha," I say, draining the bottle.

Rance signals to the barkeep.

"Lou!" he calls out, waving his hand over my empty bottle. then holds up two fingers. Lou nods in understanding and a minute later he's brought me a fresh cold one and another for Rance.

"Let's say you were interested in participating. How much participation might we be talkin' about here, Charlie?"

I shrug.

"That'd depend. Tell me about Terranova Construction."

Rance takes a deep swallow of his beer. He makes a slight face as he looks at the bottle.

"Well, it ain't Lone Star but I guess it'll do," he says. He looks back at me. "There's six of us. Limited partnership. Guess you'd say I'm the more equal among equals. The others kind of leave the details to me. Everybody's got a half-million dollars in the pot so we're capitalized at three million. We figure that'll get us most of the way there."

"Sounds to me like like you're pretty much set for money," I say.

"You'd think so but one of our boys is having a little trouble coming up with his share. No disgrace. Five hundred thousand dollars is a lot of money."

"Well, sure," I say. "For some people." Mr. Moneybags. That's me.

Rance smiles.

"You going to be around for a while, Charlie?"

"I could be," I say.

"Suppose I buy you dinner tonight at the hotel, say around seven-thirty. I'll bring along a prospectus and you can look it over whenever you get a chance."

"Sounds good," I say. "How about a chance to say hello to one or two prospective partners?"

"I'll see what I can do," Rance says.

I do the math. Seven-thirty dinner, an hour and a half to eat and if I'm lucky that puts me on the road shortly after nine and back in the city well past midnight. On the theory that maybe my business won't be finished today, I register at the hotel for one night. This chews up most of my cash since using a Joseph Bernardi check to register Charles Berger doesn't seem any too smart. Still I think it's worth it. I'm becoming more and more convinced that the events taking place in New York are rooted right here in Lakeville.

My room is on the first floor rear with a sliding glass door that leads to a private patio with a table and a couple of chairs and beyond that a swimming pool. It's not fancy but serviceable and since my only luggage is my travel kit, I'm saved the bother of unpacking. I toss the kit onto the bathroom sink counter and go out for a mini-tour of the town. The day is winding down but most of the shops are still open. I search for a red and white barber pole and spot it in the middle of the next block. I don't need a haircut but I'm going to get one anyway. In my thirty-five years I have learned one very valuable lesson. When you are in a strange place, there are two impeccable sources of information. One is a bartender, the other is the local barber.

Silvio does not disappoint me. He is a walking encyclopedia of the whos, whats, whys and hows of Lakeville. This little town doesn't need a newspaper, not as long as Silvio is around.

"Crazy people," he says dismissively."Four months ago they start. A big deal. The mayor is there to cut a ribbon. The mayor and the owners pick up shovels and dig a little. They take a lot of pictures and then they all drink a lot of champagne. You want a little more off the top?"

"No, just a trim, that's all." I say.

Gianni, his partner, who is sitting in the empty barber chair next to us waiting for the next customer, looks over critically. "You could use some off the top," he says.

"I like it the way it is," I say.

"Suit yourself," he says in a huff.

Silvio continues as if Gianni isn't even there.

"Anyway, after all this digging and drinking, six weeks later, everything stops. Zip. Boom. Nada. Everything drops dead. They're out of money. They say no, they got plenty of money. They say they're changing the layout of the course. I say 'stranzate'. Merda. You know what I mean?"

"I know what you mean," I say.

"Comes a week later, they start up again. Maybe they find some money in a cookie jar. What do I know? Most people say, okay. This is good for business, good for the town. The church people, they're not so sure. They get a—" He looks over at Gianni. "What do you call it?"

"A conjunction," Gianni says.

"That's right. They get a conjunction and shut them down. These guys want to race on Sunday. The church people say it ain't gonna happen. They go at it hot and heavy, back and forth, a lot of screamng and yelling. This lasts five days until another judge lifts this conjunction and they start clearing the land again. How long before they shut down again? Mister, your guess is as good as mine."

"Buncha crooks," Gianni mutters.

"Why do you say that?" I ask.

"I say big talk means big crooks. Like Il Duce. Il bastardo. These bandidos go around telling people they own the land. They don't own nothin'. The Vaills still own it. All these guys got is an option and from what I hear time's running out on 'em."

Now I know I've made the right decision staying the night. This million dollar enterprise is falling apart like Hitler's Thousand Year Reich.

"I'm looking for a guy," I say. "Maybe you've seen him around." I take the sketch from my pocket and show it to them. Silvio peers at it and shakes his head. Gianni takes it and gives it the once over.

"Silvio, what are you saying? You know this guy. Always hangin' around the pool hall, him and his buddies. Drives that red truck, you know, with the snake on the door."

Silvio shrugs.

"You think so? That could be a lot of guys."

"It's him. Look at the lousy haircut."

Silvio peers at it again.

"Yeah, maybe you're right," he says.

"Has he got a name?" I ask.

They shake their heads.

"Who knows from names?" Gianni says. "Half of 'em got no name at all. B.T. this, G.W. that. A.J., M.G. Once in a while a guy named Bubba. They give me five bucks, I cut their hair. That's all I want to know from these ladrones."

Ten minutes later I've bled Silvio and Gianni dry of information. Even better I've talked them into taking my fifty dollar check in return for twenty-five dollars cash. I pay them five bucks for the haircut, five bucks for a tip and I have fifteen left over for gas to get back to New York. Silvio wanted no part of this arrangement but Gianni, who I learn is Silvio's older brother, jumps at it. Maybe I have an honest face. More likely Gianni recognizes a sucker when he sees one.

I show up at the entrance to the hotel dining room at precisely seven-thirty. It's crowded but even so I spot Rance Luckett across the room at a table overlooking the rear gardens. There's another man at the table. His back is to me. The hostess approaches with a menu and I point out Rance. She leads me to the table. As I reach it Rance stands. So does the other man. He turns to face me with a smile. He's tall and thin and losing his hair. He has a long needle-like nose and eyes set close together under bushy eyebrows. The last time I saw him was Friday afternoon when he came out of a Sixth Avenue coffee shop in the company of Biff Claymore.

"Charlie Berger. Dwayne Tolliver," Rance says by way of introduction. I shake the man's hand returning his smile.

"A pleasure," he says in a deep rumbling voice.

Our waitress comes by.

"We've already ordered drinks, Charlie. What's your pleasure?" Rance says. I opt for a beer and we take our seats.

It doesn't take long for me to figure out that Tolliver is the salesman in the group. His voice is mesmerizing and he knows his product. Lime Rock is the face of tomorrow's burgeoning world of competitive auto racing. In the years to come, whether it be Formula One or Indy cars or stock cars under the banner of the National Association of Stock Car Auto Racing (NASCAR), auto racing will become the most popular, most watched sporting event in the country. Granted, to date it has mostly regional appeal with deep South venues like Daytona and Darlington and the Charlotte Fairgrounds. That's why Lime Rock is so important. It is the key to bringing auto racing into the national spotlight and there will be rich rewards for those who are among the first to become involved. I am fascinated by this guy's spiel and if I wasn't so sure he was a crook, I'd be writing him a check.

Naturally, they want to know all about me. What enterprises am I involved with? A little of this, a little of that, I tell them. Nothing I can really talk about. What the IRS doesn't know about won't hurt them. I wink. They get it. Without getting specific I tell them I hold positions in several foreign currencies, options on a half-dozen blue chips and a strong minority position in three speculative companies in the electronics field. My six office buildings in downtown Denver are more of less a sideline. Ten years of scanning The Wall Street Journal has taught me how to sling baloney with the best of them. In any case, I assure them, if I decide to become involved, I will be dealing solely in cash. I see their eyes glisten. I have uttered the magic word.

We finish off dinner with a decent brandy and an excellent Cuban cigar. This is when Rance and Dwayne decide to take me on a tour. It isn't a tour exactly. They lead me to an office at the end of one of the corridors sprouting from the lobby. The gold lettering on the glass-paned door reads "Lime Rock Race Course". Tolliver unlocks the door and flips on the lights as we enter. I am instantly impressed. In the middle of the room is a huge table upon which sits an elaborate mockup of the race track as it will look when completed. It has a rectangular oval shape like The Brickyard, two and a quarter miles in length and boasts grandstands on both sides of its two straightaways. There is ample parking for several thousand cars and a huge area near the entrance for restaurants and other concessions.

I confess to being overwhelmed which is just what they want to hear. They ask me if I am going to confer with my accountant. I laugh. I tell them that my accountant is a Nervous Nellie who wouldn't know a good investment if it fell on him. And my lawyer? I laugh again. He helps me sue people who tread on my toes. Otherwise who needs him. I have positioned myself as a clueless Rube, ready to be divested of everything but his socks and skivvies.

I look about the rest of the room. It is equally impressive. There are display shelves holding a couple of dozen first place trophies from major races down South. The walls are peppered with 8x10 photos of well known racing greats like Lee Petty, Junior Johnson,

Herb Thomas, Dick Rathmann and Johnny Mantz. And interspersed are group shots of the various racing teams. I spot Rance's photo and below it the group shot of the men who work for him. I walk over for a closer look. The caption reads: Team Luckett-Durham, North Carolina."

"Nice photo, Rance," I say. "You're in good company."

"I've won my share," he says.

My eyes drop down to the group shot which is when I see him. There are six men in his crew. The tall guy on the end has long dark sideburns, black greasy hair, and a thin pencil mustache. I lean in for a closer look. I don't think there's any question. This is the guy. I glance at the identifying caption below the photo. His name is Ethan Goodbody. It's a name I'm not likely to forget.

"See anybody you like?"

I turn sharply. Rance is standing directly behind me, staring at me hard, as hard as I was staring at the group photo.

CHAPTER FOURTEEN

"Your gang?" I say, tapping the photo.

"My gang," Rance says flatly, his eyes never leaving mine.

"Fantastic!" I say, shaking my head in wonderment. "You know how some kids grow up wanting to run away to the circus. Not me. All I could think about from the time I was five years old was cars, cars, cars. Fix 'em, drive 'em, race 'em. My old man, he was a dirt farmer, he thought I was crazy. His idea of something really special and exciting was an eighty pound pumpkin. When he died, I buried him in the pumpkin patch. Seemed like a good idea at the time."

Slowly I move away from the photo. I can feel Rance's eyes boring in on me. Then I turn and look around the room.

"Special. Very special," I say, stretching my arms feigning weariness. "But right now I'm bushed after that long drive up from New York. I'm going to turn in." I walk to the door. "Why don't you boys draw up some partnership papers and we can talk about them over breakfast."

"Excellent idea, Charlie. We'll meet you in the dining room around nine," Rance says.

"Looking forward to it," Dwayne Tolliver says with a smile.

I amble down the corridor, cross the lobby and head down the hallway to my room which is on the other side of the building. Fat chance that I'll be showing up for breakfast at nine. Fat chance that I'll even be in the hotel. I unlock my door and go in, shut it and throw the safety lock. I flip on the lights and cross over to the television set which I turn on. I don't touch the tuner because I really don't care what's on but I do make sure the volume is high. I go to my sliding door and look out. It's dark now. There's a half-moon tonight but also low hanging rain clouds. Plenty of cover for what I have in mind. I pull the drapes shut, then retrieve my travel kit from the bathroom. I check my watch. 9:43. I take one last look around. The scene is set. I've retired for the night and am watching a little television before sleep claims me. Quickly I move to the drapes and step behind them, opening the sliding door just enough to slip through onto my patio. Quietly I close the door behind me. I move a few feet to my left and take up a position behind some shrubs. I stand very still and watch and listen. The clouds continue to obscure the moon. I hold that pose for well over a minute until I'm sure I've left my room unobserved.

Convinced that I have not been spotted, I begin to make my way to the parking lot, keeping to the shadows of the building and the shrubbery. When I am directly across from the section where I parked my car, I step out into the open and walk casually toward the lot. My eyes flit in every direction and see nothing out of place. Two minutes later I'm standing by the driver's side door and am about to insert the key into the lock when I hear his voice behind me.

"Going somewhere, Charlie?"

I turn, startled. Rance Luckett is at the car in the next row, leaning against the trunk, a revolver in his hand and a bemused smile on his lips.

I try to think fast.

"Got a splitting headache and I ran out of aspirin. There's a late night drug store a few blocks away."

"Hotel gift shop sells aspirin," Rance says.

"They closed at nine."

"Did they? Too bad. But I think you can get those little packages of two from the concierge."

"Can you? I didn't know," I say. "Is there some reason you're pointing that gun at me?"

"Yes, there is. As long as you're out here why don't we drive over to the druggist and get your aspirin."

I shake my head.

"Not really necessary. I'm feeling better " I start to turn away from the car door.

"Unlock it, open the door and get behind the wheel, Mr. Bernardi."

Uh,oh, He knows my real name.This shows signs of getting real messy real soon.

"Look, I—uh—"

"The door, Bernardi. Now."

He steps toward me, gun aimed squarely at my belly. I consider my options and conclude that I don't have any. I open the door and slide behind the wheel.

"Hands on the steering wheel where I can see them and don't do anything stupid," he says as he circles in front of the car and comes around to the passenger door. He opens it and slides in next to me. The gun never wavers.

"Let's go," he says.

I put the key in the ignition, start the engine and flip on the headlights. I pull forward and turn toward the entrance of the parking lot and as I do, my beams light up the pick up truck sitting a few yards ahead of me, motor idling quietly. It's red. There is a coiled snake painted on the driver's side door. Behind the wheel is a man. I can't see his face but I don't need to. I know who it is.

"Drive," Rance says.

"And if I don't?" I say.

He cocks the hammer with a shrug.

"Makes no difference to me," he replies.

Suddenly driving seems like a good idea. I pull forward to the street.

"Turn right," Rance says.

"Drug store's to the left."

"Turn right."

I do as I'm told. As I start down the street I look in my rear view and watch as the red truck slides in behind us a couple of car lengths back.

"We can make this easy," Rance says, "or we can make it very painful so before I turn you over to Ethan, where's the woman?"

"What woman?" I ask. On a scale of one to ten this is probably the stupidest response I could come up with.

"Oh, Lord," Rance sighs, "this is going to get really ugly." We've come to an intersection. "Straight," he says. I continue on.

"Look, Bernardi," Rance says, "I know nothing about you except that you're nosy and probably a lot dumber than you look. If you were smart you wouldn't be risking your miserable life for some two-bit hooker."

I don't know how to respond to that so I keep my mouth shut. In fact I'm so busy trying to figure a way out of this mess that I'm only half listening to him.

"Ethan has nothing against you personally and you sure as hell don't pose a threat to him. His only problem is the woman and as soon as he takes care of her, you're free to shoot off your mouth to anybody who'll listen because the truth is, you don't know squat and for sure not anything you can prove."

"You mean, like who hired him to kill Daphne Gennaro?" I say.

Rance shakes his head in disbelief.

"Now there you go," he says. "I just get finished telling you that you're safe because you don't know anything and you ask a question that could get you killed. What's with you, boy? Were you raised by chipmunks or something? Right at the next corner."

The intersection looms up. I turn right. The red truck is right on my tail. I pass a sign which reads "Wononskopomuc Lake—1 Mile". I suspect this is an Indian word meaning 'So long,sucker'.

"I was pretty sure that Harvey Junior was behind Daphne's killing but not any more," I tell him. "You and your boy back there have convinced me it had everything to do with money and lots of it."

"You just won't quit, will you?" Rance says.

"One of my many failings," I say as we pass a sign identifying the road we're on as Rte. 44. "Tell me about Biff Claymore."

"What about him?"

"I understand he's part of the gang," I say.

"Not yet. Five hundred thousand makes you one of the boys. So far all we've seen from Claymore is fifty thousand and that buys you nothing but your name on the list. He's got a few more days, then we keep his fifty and move on."

"Then I guess you must have a helluva lot of people clamoring to get in on this solid gold investment." He gives me a cold look. "There's a dirt road coming up on the right that leads to the lake. Take it," Rance says.

I don't think so, I tell myself. On Rte. 44, I have a chance, albeit a slim one, to attract enough attention to save my hide. At the edge of Lake Unpronouncable, my only allies will be hoot owls and bunny rabbits. I tromp hard on the gas pedal.The car shoots forward leaving the lake turnoff behind us. I was told the Ford Victoria V/8 had power. I'm about to find out.

"Hey!" Rance yells. "What the hell are you doing?"

"Going for a spin," I say.

"Slow down!" he says sharply, pointing the gun at my head. I glance at the speedometer. It's past 65 and heading for 70. The road is unlit and at times curvy with huge trees growing at both sides of the road. Visibility is intermittent as the moon keeps coming in and out of the cloud cover. "You want to shoot, then shoot."

"I'm warning you—!"

"Warn me all you like. Pull the trigger and take your chances. You got the guts for it, Rance?" 75 going on 80. The tires are squealng now every time I vary from straight ahead.

"You're going to get us killed!" I hear the panic in his voice. I don't dare look over at him. I'm not a good driver and I have a white-knuckle grip on the wheel. I can't risk taking my eyes off the road, even for a split second. One mistake, one overreaction and I could put us into a giant oak tree. I don't even glance up into the rear view mirror but I don't have to. Peripherally I'm aware of the truck's headlights behind us. I'm not outrunning him. A sign looms up on my right. 'Salisbury 5 Miles".

"How expendable are you, Rance?" I ask him.

"What are you talking about?"

"I mean, when Ethan gets tired of chasing us and tries to force us off the road, there's a good chance one or both of us will be killed. How does that sit with you?"

Tree branches overhang the road and I'm am driving straight down a long dark tunnel. I'm lightheaded, as if experiencing an out of body episode. Suddenly a young deer darts across the road a few yards in front of us. Rance screams in terror. I tweak the wheel just enough to miss him as we fly by. The speedometer is pushing 90. Up ahead I see taillights. I'm rapidly catching up with a slow moving station wagon. As I start to climb up his rear end I start flicking my high beams and blowing my horn and then an instant later I pull out and pass him. I don't look over but I sense he has passengers with him. I hear him blasting his horn at me. Good. Maybe he'll stop somewhere and call the cops. A quick glance into the rear view. The red pickup has flown by the wagon and is starting to gain on me. My eyes zero in on the gas gauge. The needle is hovering on the wrong side of E. What next? A flat tire? I can't slow down to take a turn even if I wanted to. I can only pray I get to Salisbury and civilization before my tank runs dry and even if I do that's no guarantee Rance won't pull the trigger once I've slowed to a stop.

And then I see it. About a hundred yards in front of me on the right side of the road. Lights. People. Several parked cars. I'm not sure what it is but if I'm lucky it's salvation. As I draw closer I get a good look at the back end of the nearest car. A sign is affixed to the trunk. "Just Married". A gaggle of tin cans is tied to the rear bumper. A couple of young people are nearby, kissing and embracing a dozen or more well-wishers. There are cars alongside the road and more cars parked in the driveway but as I fly toward the scene in front of me, I see a narrow opening in the shrubs that opens up onto a broad expanse of lawn. I turn the wheel and plow through the greenery, speeding out onto the lawn and chewing up grass in the process. I hear screams coming from the roadside guests as I hit the brake and start to turn the wheel. Bad idea. Too little braking. Too much turning. I feel the car give way as it cuts through the grass, then I'm up on two wheels and suddenly we're in the air and rolling over. The car slams down in its roof as I clutch at the wheel to prevent being tossed about like a rag doll in a tornado. I hear a grunt of pain coming from Rance and then we are rolling over, once, twice before the car comes to a stop on it's side. I am being squashed under Rance's weight. I think maybe he is dead or unconcious but no, he's moving, struggling to reach up to his door. He squats, half standing, his shoe in my neck as he manages to get his door open and pulls himself up and out of the front seat. I struggle to get up. Through the windshield I can see the people approaching us, some cautiously, some running. At that moment I see Rance, pistol in hand. He raises it over his head and fires into the air. More screaming as the people scatter. He turns and hobbling badly, limps across the lawn toward the street where the red pickup has stopped. Ethan has gotten out and is helping Rance to the truck. He shoves him into the cab and slams the door and then hurries around to the driver's side. In a moment the truck is speeding away down the darkened highway.

Inside the car I struggle to raise myself up. Suddenly hands are reaching down to me and pulling me up and out of the car. People are shouting and firing questions at me. I try to maintain my balance but I can't. I feel myself falling. I hear someone suggest they call the police. I start to raise my hand to second the motion but instead I pass out.

Now it's nearly midnight. The guests have all left and the newlyweds are on their way to Nirvana if they haven't been there already. The man of the house, Quentin Hardisty, has me sitting at his kitchen table and is plying me with coffee and left over hors d'oeuvres from the party. His wife Ethel has gone to bed. The excitement has been too much for her. Quentin is a really nice guy and a lot more charitable than I might be in similar circumstances. He is fascinated by my story which he says sounds just like a movie. It doesn't hurt that I tell him I am actually friends with people like Bogart and Cagney.

The cop's name is Michael Whitefeather and I suspect he is of Indian descent, partly because of his name but mostly because he can pronounce the name of the lake. The brownish skin tone, high cheekbones and sleek jet black hair confirm my suspicions. He is the resident trooper for the Connecticut State Police assigned to Salisbury and in the absence of any kind of county sheriff's department, he is what passes for law and order in this underpopulated corner of the state.

"What kind of a gun did you say it was?" Michael asks, pad and pencil at the ready.

"Loaded," I say. Michael frowns.

"That sort of response is not helpful, Mr. Bernardi," he says to me.

"I guess not but that's the third time you've asked me that question and since you don't seem to be satisfied with 'I don't know'. I thought I'd try something different. And why aren't you out on the streets looking for those guys?"

"Because I'm sitting here with you taking your statement and because by this time, they could be half way to Bangor, Maine." He waves his notepad at me. "I have it all here, Mr. Bernardi. Rance Luckett. Ethan Goodbody. Red pickup truck with a snake on the door. That's all been phoned in to headquarters. If they're still in Connecticut, we'll get them."

Quentin Hardisty has brought the coffee pot over from the stove.

"More coffee, Sergeant?"

Michael waves him off.

"No, thanks."

"Joe?"

I shake my head.

"I'm good, thanks," I tell him, nibbling at a Ritz cracker with cream cheese and an olive slice on it.

"I take it you two have worked out what to do about the car out on the lawn," Michael says.

"No problem," Hardisty says.

"I took the insurance when I rented it," I say. "I'll call them first thing in the morning and everything should be taken care of. What isn't I'll write a check for."

Michael nods and flips his notepad shut.

"Well, I guess that's it then, " he says. "Mr. Bernardi, you're free to go."

"Go? Go where?" I ask in disbelief.

"I don't know," Michael says. "Back to your hotel room?"

"Sergeant, there are two murderous bastards running around looking for me. Does that sound like the hotel's a good idea?"

"No, no, of course not. You're right."

"You're welcome to stay the night here, Joe," Hardisty says.

"Thanks, Quent," I say, "but I'm dangerous to be around right now. Better I spend the night in one of the sergeant's jail cells."

"I have no cause to hold you," Michael says.

"Suppose I punch you in the nose. Would that do it?"

"Yes, but—"

"Then let's pretend I did."

"Have it your way," Michael sighs as he gets up from the table. I follow suit and again thank Hardisty for his understanding and cooperation. I give him my card and tell him to call me any time day or night if he runs into any problems.

It takes the sergeant and me less than ten minutes to get to his little hole-in-the-wall office in the middle of Salisbury. Inside I'm introduced to Shawna Cafferty who mans the desk and the phones during the graveyard hours. Michael leads me to the three holding cells at the back of the office. The doors are all open. Take your pick, he tells me. I try all three but I'm no Goldilocks. I can't find a mattress that's just right so I flop down on the last one I try. It's probably better than the floor but only slightly. Michael wishes me a good night and leaves.

I lay back, my head on a skimpy pillow and look up at the ceiling. For the next few hours I should be relatively safe. All I really need is a good night's sleep. Just then a worrisome thought creeps into my mind. I try to remember whether or not I saw a holstered gun on Shawna's hip and I think maybe I didn't. My eyes are wide open. I don't feel as if they're going to close any time soon. I relive the horror of the car crash without the adrenalin and as I do, tiny little aches begin to infest every part of my body. I pray for sleep. My prayers go unanswered.

CHAPTER FIFTEEN

I awaken to the smell of hot brewed coffee and the sound of my cell door squeaking open. I pop open one eye and see Shawna standing over me holding a tray. Breakfast, she says with a smile. Gingerly I swing my legs to the floor and sit up. Coffee, juice, toast, bacon and eggs. I'm surprised and grateful and thank her profusely. She shakes her head and says it's nothing. There's a diner across the street that opens early on Sunday mornings. We do the same for wife beaters, she says, but she winks and I'm pretty sure she's kidding. As she walks back into her office I see she's wearing a formidable pistol on her hip. Belatedly I'm relieved. I cautiously try to stretch out the kinks and get rewarded with stabs of pain in my shoulders, back, and neck. The tossing around I endured in the car wreck is making itself felt.

Sergeant Mike arrives around nine o'clock. He tells me he's already been to the Monarch Hotel in Lakeville where there has been no sign of Luckett or Goodbody since last evening. Nor has there been a sighting by any police entity in the state so if they are still around they are keeping out of sight. Personally the sergeant thinks it most likely they have fled Connecticut. I wonder, with some trepidation, if they have fled it for New York City.

Shawna has already let me use the phone to make some vital phone calls. The car rental agency has been notified and someone from their Hartford operation will arrange to pick up the wreck and have it towed back to the capitol. I gave them the Hotel Astor as a contact number if they needed to reach me. I also called the Smith-Lerner Hospital in White Plains and spoke to Dr. Anders. Personal contact with a patient is not allowed during the first week but she told me that Bunny is doing exceptionally well, participating in group sessions, and cooperating in every way. I couldn't have asked for a better report.

Finally I called Sergeant Horvath at the Ninth Precinct. The desk sergeant told me he wasn't on duty today but if it was urgent he'd get him a message. I said it was and he said he would. That's why, when the phone rang at quarter past nine, I suspected it was Horvath getting back to me and when Shawna handed the receiver to me, I was sure of it.

"Hi," I say.

"Hi? What do you mean, hi? State police?"

"Calm down, Sarge. First things first. How's Vicki doing?"

"Terrific. They may let her go home tomorrow. Now where the hell are you and what are you up to?"

"Right now I'm having coffee with the sergeant in charge after having spent the night in a jail cell."

"What? Jesus Christ, Bernardi—!"

"Relax. I'm fine," I say. "A few cuts and scrapes, minor bruises although the car is a total wreck."

"What car? Where are you?"

"State Police Office, Salisbury, Connecticut. I'm stuck here without transportation, no money and no way to get any and I need a ride back to New York City."

"Is that why you called me? To hitch a ride?" Horvath asks. I can hear his blood pressure rising.

"Sure, and also to fill you in on information vital to your murder investigation."

"Such as?"

"First the ride," I say.

Silence. Then: "I have a good mind to leave you there."

"But you won't."

More silence.

"Where'd you say you were? Salisbury? Where is that?" Horvath asks.

"Buy yourself a map, Sarge. See you around noon."

I hang up. At six minutes to twelve a black Ford sedan with a whip antenna and New York plates pulls up in front of the office. Horvath gets out of the car wearing his off-duty Sunday best: Levis, a Brooklyn Dodgers sweatshirt and an NYPD baseball cap. When I step out of the office to greet him, he looks none too happy to see me. He'd forgotten he'd promised to take his wife and the two kids for a Central Park picnic this afternoon and now his name is atop a list his wife keeps to chronicle his domestic infractions. He explains that getting on the list is relatively easy. Getting off takes an act of Congress. I pretend to care but the truth is, I've almost gotten myself killed doing his job for him. He'll get no sympathy from me.

I thank Michael and Shawna for their help and tell them how I can be reached. Horvath and I are on the road by twelve-eighteen and for the first twenty minutes, his irritated silence speaks volumes. I lean back in my seat, eyes closed. If he wants to be pissy, let him. I have lots of time and infinite patience.

Finally he can't stand it any more.

"Okay, so what's this vital information you're keeping from me?" he says.

"How about the identity of the man who shot and killed Daphne Gennaro in the jail cell?"

"You know who he is?"

"I do."

"Well?"

"First you'll have to admit it was certainly a good idea that I made this trip."

He takes his eyes off the road long enough to glare at me. I smile at him.

"Okay, it was a good idea,:" he grumbles reluctantly.

"And I'm not really out of my mind."

"Right. You're not out of your mind," he mumbles.

"Sorry," I say. "Didn't hear that."

"Maybe you'd like it in writing," Horvath growls loudly.

"Not necessary."

He glares at me again.

"Maybe you'd like to walk the rest of the way to New York."

"Okay,okay," I say. "Truce?"

"Truce," he replies.

For the next thirty minutes I fill him in. I tell him about Ethan Goodbody who is without a doubt the triggerman who killed Daphne Gennaro. As to who might have ordered him to do it, that's another story. I describe as best I can the Lime Rock operation including my opinion that the whole thing is being run by a bunch of incompetents or it's some kind of gigantic scam. I suggest that the man holding the gun on Dr. Hatfield while Goodbody was being patched up was probably Rance Luckett or maybe even Dwayne Tolliver, the syrup-voiced snake oil salesman. I go into detail about the wild car chase along darkened roads the night before and my deliberate crashing of the car in the middle of the wedding party followed by the escape of Luckett and Goodbody in the red pickup truck. I tell Horvath that an APB is out for the men and the vehicle but so far no sign of either.

When I finish he glances over at me.

"You were busy," he says.

"I was."

"And you are insane. Insane and lucky to be alive."

"You bet your ass," I say. "Now here's what I suggest."

"I can't wait to hear it," Horvath replies.

"Luckett's racing team is centered in Durham, North Carolina, so it might be useful to check with the police there and get a line on him, his operation, and the people who work for him, particularly Ethan Goodbody."

"That's your suggestion?" Horvath asks.

"Yes."

"Well, it isn't half bad," he says grudgingly. "If you ever decide to get a real job, I might find an opening for you."

I grin.

"Thanks, Sarge. That's the nicest thing anyone's ever said to me. When we get back to New York I'm going to call your wife and tell her that you saved my life."

Horvath looks at me glumly.

"It won't help."

We're back in New York by three and Horvath drops me off at the Astor. I check at the front desk and switch to yet another room in an abundance of caution just in case Luckett and Goodbody have not yet given up on me. I register under the name Marty Piletti which is Ernie Borgnine's character name in the movie. Anyone asking for Marty gets put right through. If a caller asks for me, they are to say I'm out and take a name and a phone number.

Once inside my new room, I take three aspirin, slip out of my shoes, flop down on the bed and crash. When I awaken. it's dark out. I look at my watch. Nearly eight-thirty. That makes it five-thirty Pacific time. No sense putting it off any longer. I walk over to the phone in the desk and buzz the hotel operator.

Three minuted later a familiar voice comes on the line.

"Hello."

"Hi. It's me," I say.

"Well, thanks for the call, stranger," Jill says sarcastically. "You leave town Tuesday without a word and let me stew for five days wondering where you are."

"New York," I say. "You could have asked Glenda Mae."

"I tried that. She was strangely uncommunicative."

"She takes her job as gatekeeper very seriously," I say.

"Not with business trips, Joe, and certainly not with me. This is a business trip, isn't it?"

I hesitate.

"Mostly," I say.

"And the leftover part?"

"Personal."

"Personal as in 'None of your business'? If so, it's okay as long as you're okay."

"It's about Bunny, Jill," I say.

There's a moment's silence.

"All right," she says quietly.

I tell her about Bunny's call to Ginger Tate and Ginger's call to me. I tell her about the church shelter and Sister Veronica Marie and the A.A. meetings nearby and Bunny's desperate need to get into a rehabilitation program. I don't tell her about the murder in the police station or my involvement in trying to protect her. I also omit any mention of Connecticut. No sense worrying her. There's nothing she can do.

"The hospital. Were you able to get her into the program?" she asks.

"I was and I'm told she's doing fine."

"Good," she says. "You said it was what, a sixty day program?"

"Something like that."

"Are you planning to spend the whole sixty days in New York?"

"Of course not," I say.

"I just thought—."

"I have a job, Jill. She's in good hands at the hospital."

"I'm sure she is. Will you be there when she's released?"

"I don't know. Maybe. Look, I don't think this is something we should be discussing on the phone."

"Of course, you're right," she says. "Forgive me."

"Jill, there's nothing to forgive."

"Sorry. Bad choice of words. When will you be coming back to L.A.?"

"I don't know. I'm tied up with this movie. We talked about it. Marty."

"The old TV show."

"That's the one."

"I thought you said it was a silly idea." Her inflection is cool and accusatory.

"I did. I may have been wrong."

"That was a quick change of mind," she says. Her voice is becoming even cooler. I think she wants to start a fight. I won't let her.

"Jill, it's great to hear your voice. I've really missed you. I'll call you in a day or two when I have a better sense of my schedule. Love to the baby."

And I hang up. I'm glad there are three thousand miles between us. The call went about the way I thought it would. Bunny is Jill's demon and always will be. I think for a moment about supper but I haven't the energy to leave the room or the patience to deal with room service. I grab an apple from a bowl on my dresser and take a healthy bite. I get back in bed, propping myself up with a couple of pillows, my thoughts turning to Ethan Goodbody. For days he has been the elusive answer to the question "Who?" Now I realize that there is an even more perplexing question and that is "Why?" Why does a man like Goodbody who has everything to do with the machinations at Lime Rock walk into a police station and murder in cold blood a woman with whom he has no obvious connection? Who hired him? Harvey Junior certainly had a motive. Maybe even Harvey Senior but neither of them had a connection to the racing crowd. Biff Claymore was in hip deep with the Lime Rockers but what did that have to do with Daphne Gennaro? Certainly nothing obvious.

Now I'm getting a headache to go along with my other aches and pains. I dig up three more aspirin which I toss down my throat followed by another bite of apple. I have to stop my mind from dwelling on these irrelevancies. I have only one objective that means anything. Find Ethan Goodbody before he finds Bunny. Everything else is immaterial.

CHAPTER SIXTEEN

The cab drops me off at a twelve story office building on the corner of Seventh Avenue and 48th Street. It's been around quite a while but not so long that it's become a dilapidated eyesore. On the fourth floor are the offices of Anselm Forsythe III and if anyone can tell me where I can find Biff Claymore, it's Anselm. I've decided that Biff is the one most likely to be acquainted with Ethan Goodbody and therefore may know where I can find him. I know it's a longshot but at the moment I have nothing else.

I exit the elevator and walk along the dimly lit corridor looking for Suite 422. I locate it halfway down and pause in front of the door. The gilt lettering on the door reads "Anselm Forsythe III and Associates. Attorney at Law". Associates? Didn't know he had any. Even though the lettering warns me "By Referral Only", I grasp the doorknob and walk in.

If this be a suite, then I be Louis B. Mayer. And if this place was recently refurbished by a swanky Park Avenue decorator, then someone should be in line for a massive refund. I'm looking at a tiny outer office, barely large enough for a desk and chair which at the moment are not in use. To the left is the small private office of Anselm Forsythe III. I can tell because the door is open and he is bent over some paperwork. chewing on the end of a pencil. I look around for the associates but none are in sight.

I walk over to his office door and knock on the jamb. He looks up, startled. I expect him to smile and invite me in. He doesn't.

"I'm a little busy now, Mr. Bernardi," he says to me.

"So am I, Anselm, but this won't take long. Your receptionist must be on a coffee break," I say nodding my head toward his ante room.

"She's taken a couple of days off," he says.

"Must be more than a couple judging by the depth of the dust on her desk out there," I say.

"Look, I am very busy getting ready to file Lila Claymore's last will and testament. I have no time to chat."

"Then I'll make it quick. Where can I find Biff Claymore?"

"That would be confidential, Mr. Bernardi," he says.

"Okay," I say, pulling up a chair. "Then I'll just stick around until it's in public domain."

Forsythe glowers at me.

"If you don't leave, I will call the police."

I reach for my wallet.

"Let me help you out. I have Sergeant Horvath's number right here." I make a big show of sorting through the contents of my billfold.

Forsythe shakes his head with a sigh.

"All right. You win." He takes a leatherbound book from his desk and flips it open, then gives me an address on the upper West Side of the city. "As his attorney, may I ask why you seem so anxious to reach him?"

"Sure, I have a lot of questions I want to ask him about Lime Rock." Forsythe's eyes narrow. I've jarred him. "You know about that," I say.

"His interest in that race course is no secret, Mr. Bernardi. In fact it has caused a serious rift between Biff and his father."

"And whose side are you on?" I ask.

"I beg your pardon."

"You just told me you were Biff Claymore's attorney. You're also his father's attorney. Don't they call that conflict of interest?"

"It can be. It isn't."

"That's convenient. Did you have anything to do with arranging for his financial position in the operation?"

"None of your concern."

"Then let me put it another way. Did you manage to scout up fifty thousand dollars for him to make an initial payment? Somebody sure did and I doubt it was his father."

"I suggest you direct your questions to young Mr. Claymore."

"Good idea. How well do you know Ethan Goodbody?"

"Who?"

"Tall, dark and not really handsome, usually seen in the company of lethal weapons."

"I don't know who you're talking about."

"Rance Luckett. Dwayne Tolliver."

His eyes narrow. He responds cautiously.

"What about them?"

"You tell me."

"I believe Biff once mentioned their names as investors in the Lime Rock venture. That's all I know about either one of them. What is the purpose of all these questions, Mr. Bernardi, and more to the point, what business is this of yours?"

"I'm hot on the trail of an unprincipled cold blooded killer, Mr. Forsythe. Seeing as you are a lawyer, I thought you might know him."

It probably takes a lot to get Anselm Forsythe III enraged but I'm pretty sure I've brought him to the boiling point.

"Get out," he says quietly.

I hesitate.

"Sure. Sorry to have spoiled your morning. If I think of anything else I need to know I'll be back."

I start for the open doorway but when I get there, I turn back.

"One last question," I say.

"Ask it, then go."

"Mrs. Claymore's will. Did she make any provisions for her sons or did her husband get it all?"

"Goodbye, Mr. Bernardi."

"Sergeant Horvath can get a subpoena in a heartbeat, counselor, and you know it. Do we have to go through all that trouble when I am standing here in the doorway ready to leave?"

Forsythe considers his options. My leaving is the one he likes best.

"Mr. Claymore Senior inherited everything. Neither son was mentioned.

"Cross your heart?" I say.

"Goodbye, Mr. Bernardi," Forsythe says yet again and this time I make his day. I leave.

In the elevator on the way to street level, I feel a slight pang of disappointment. The moment Forsythe mentioned Lila Forsythe's will, a thought started to germinate in my brain and it had to do with that mysterious fifty thousand dollars that Biff was able to produce to buy his way into the Lime Rock operation. I don't know him well enough to suspect him of matricide but I do know that his desire to become a part of Lime Rock borders on obsession. Forsythe's revelation pretty much negates that avenue of exploration. I say pretty much because there is always the outside chance that Biff mistakenly believed he was an heir to his mother's estate. This is something I really hate thinking about. A man is not supposed to kill his mother. Hallmark says so.

It takes me five minutes to flag down an empty cab and another twenty to reach Biff's apartment house on West 48th Street. There's no doorman so I surmise the rent's on the cheap side. Inside there's a lobby and a security desk. I reconsider. The rent may not be as cheap as I thought. The guy at the desk whose name tag reads 'Jonas' is beefy with a flattop hair cut and a ramrod bearing and I guess former M.P. I tell him I'm here to see Biff Claymore. He asks if I am expected and I tell him no. In that case, Jonas tells me, he is unavailable. Does that mean he is in, out, asleep, awake or what? Unavailable, Jonas repeats. Just then the elevator door opens and a blowsy young woman in a badly wrinkled satin dress and matching high heels marches out and heads for the entrance. Her hair is a mess as is her makeup and the set of her jaw is formidable. Jonas watches her go. I watch Jonas watching her and when he looks back at me, I say, "Does that mean he might suddenly be a little more available?"

"I doubt it," Jonas says.

"She didn't look any too happy," I say.

"Probably stiffed her on the tip. He's like that," Jonas says with a sneer in his voice.

"I'm not," I say, laying two 20's on his desk. I replenished my money supply with the hotel cashier.

"He doesn't like me calling up before noon," Jonas says, unable to take his eyes off the two Jacksons.

"Make an exception."

I give him my name and he makes the call. He turns his back to me and speaks quietly, finally turning around and hanging up.

"He has no interest in speaking to you," Jonas says, scooping up the bills.

I nod.

"Over the past several weeks, has he had an unusual visitors? I'm thinking specifically of a guy who drives a red pickup truck."

"Sorry, bud. All Mr. Claymore's visitors wear skirts. They come at night and they leave in the morning. As far as that truck goes, I've never seen it."

"What about going out? Does he ever leave the apartment?" I ask

"Sure," Jonas says. "Two or three afternoons a week. He likes to hang around Lou Stillman's gym. For a while he thought about becoming a boxer, even took a few lessons, but I think now he just likes to watch. They all train there, you know. Sugar Ray, LaMotta, Ezzard, Jersey Joe, Graziano. All of them."

I thank him and leave. If I am to speak with Biff Claymore it will be some other place at some other time. The idea of the gym sounds promising. I'll have to check it out. When I hit the street I look for a place likely to have a telephone and find it at a small local grocery store. I grab a buck's worth of change from the clerk and call Horvath.

"I was hoping you'd call," he says when he comes on the line.

"Good news?" I ask.

"Depends on how you look at it," he says. "A couple of officers in Brooklyn stumbled across the red pickup truck. They had it impounded this morning. Looks like your boys are here in the city."

"Guess I'd better watch my back," I say.

"I would if I were you," Horvath replies. "Especially after what I learned from the police chief in Durham."

"Tell me."

"Your pal, Ethan Goodbody, is a stone cold killer. Four arrests involving corpses, three mistrials and one conviction for manslaughter. Four years in state prison. Even his mother's afraid of him."

"What about his father?

"That was mistrial number one. He was seventeen years old."

"Lovely."

"About Rance Luckett. He's a small timer and a perpetual loser. He's entered a few decent sized races but most people in the area think he's a joke. He made his money bootlegging and the chief thinks he's still at it. He idolizes all the big racing guys, wants to be one of them. No way it's going to happen, the Chief says. and Luckett probably knows it."

"And Dwayne Tolliver?"

"Used to be a lawyer. The Chief thinks he got himself disbarred as a result of a conviction in New York sixteen years ago for passing bad checks."

"That'd do it," I say.

"Did fourteen months at Rikers. In any case he gave up his practice. These days he seems to be into a lot of things, mostly borderline legal."

"So maybe Lime Rock is a scam."

"Maybe so," Horvath says. "I don't know enough about it. Anyway I have a city-wide APB out on Goodbody and Luckett. We may get lucky and pick them up."

"Let's hope," I say.

I say goodbye and hang up. I suppose I'm happy the two men are here in the city. Better to confront them now than have them sneak up on me or Bunny two or three years down the line when we least expect it. I step out onto the street into the sunlight. It's nearing noon and I should be hungry. I had a bagel and coffee breakfast but my adrenalin is pumping and there is something I have to check on before I eat.

I hail a passing cab and hop into the back seat.

"Times Square," I tell him.

The New York Times morgue is one of the largest and most complete in the country. It's where dead stories go to be microfiched instead of ending up at the bottom of a parakeet cage. I check at the information desk just inside the main entrance and learn from the helpful young lady on duty that I actually don't want the morgue, I want the first floor reading room where copies of the last thirty days of the Times editions are available for perusal. It's a huge room with plenty of tables and chairs as well as sofas and easy chairs. Along the walls are racks of back dated copies of the newspaper, all of them mounted on three foot wooden poles, the better to prevent pilferers from walking away with a paper secreted beneath a trench coat.

I systematically start looking and within ten minutes I have found what I am after. I sit down at one of the tables and spread out the paper. From my pocket I take out a small notepad and a pencil. The paper is dated August 28 and the article is on the first page of the second section. There is a flattering photo of Lila Claymore who is described as a society matron deeply involved in city charities dealing with the homeless and destitute. The headline reads "Lila Claymore, Philanthropist, Killed in Accident" and the article includes quotes from the investigative officers and several eyewitnesses. There are a few inconsistencies but there are certain points on which all agreed. First, she was crossing the street legally in a crosswalk with the light. Secondly, the vehicle that struck her seemed to come out of nowhere and appeared to be making a deliberate effort to hit her. Third, the vehicle was a red pickup truck with round slap-on decals affixed to both front doors identifying the owner as "Brown's Bakery". Fourth, the man behind the wheel was wearing a baseball cap and sunglasses. And fifth, the front and rear license plates were spattered with mud and unreadable. However two witnesses were sure the plates were out-of-state based on the colors that were visible.

I write all of this down in my little notepad and then I replace the newspaper in the rack. I go in search of a telephone and when I find it, I call Sergeant Horvath.

When he picks up, I say to him, "About that red pickup truck you've got impounded in Brooklyn....."

CHAPTER SEVENTEEN

"Kind Hearts and Coronets."

"What?

"Kind Hearts and Coronets."

"What the hell is that?" Horvath asks.

"A movie," I reply.

"Never saw it."

"Made in England around 1949."

"Darn. Just missed it," Horvath says trying to return his attention to the pile of paperwork on his desk. I'm sitting opposite him trying desperately to get him to pay attention to what I'm saying. "Dennis Price plays this nobody who by some quirk of fate is actually ninth in line for a British title as well as the huge fortune that goes with it."

"Uh-huh." Horvath says, half-listening.

"Alec Guiness plays all eight characters that stand between Price and the title and the plot is this. Price systematically goes about killing all eight of them so that finally he is the only living claimant to the title."

"And your point is?"

"Biff Claymore," I say.

"What about him?"

"Biff Claymore is killing off everybody who stands between him and the Claymore estate. Not personally. He's having it done by Ethan Goodbody but he's behind it."

Horvath puts down his pencil and stares me in the eyes.

"That's a pretty wild accusation, Joe," he says. "Where's your proof?"

"Don't have any yet but it explains a lot of things. For example, why Goodbody ran down Lila Claymore on a New York street. More to the point, it answers the question, why shoot Daphne Gennaro? Because she was carrying Harvey Junior's child making her kid a possible claimant to the estate."

"Farfetched."

"You think so? Three weeks ago Lila was run down on the street. A week ago Daphne is shot and killed and three days ago Harvey Junior supposedly jumps out a window and kills himself. You want farfetched? There's your farfetched. You need to pick up Biff Claymore immediately."

"On what charge?"

"I don't know," I say, "How about consorting with hookers?"

Horvath raises his eyes heavenward.

"Oh, God, deliver me from amateurs. And shall I also arrest the Deputy Mayor, Joe? Same charge. I can, you know. He's a busy little boy with a kinky disposition."

'Take me seriously, Sarge. I know I'm right."

"Hell, Joe, maybe you are, but I have absolutely zero grounds for questioning Biff Claymore, let alone taking him into custody. You're probably not aware of this but the ACLU is on the warpath again. All criminals are downtrodden misguided victims of a cruel society. All police are fascist thugs only one step removed from Hitler's Gestapo. You want me to go after Biff Claymore, better bring me reasonable cause."

I get up.

"Well, I'm not going to sit around waiting for something to happen," I say.

"Nobody here is just sitting around," Horvath says sharply. "We got photos by fax from Durham of both Goodbody and Luckett and they've been distributed all over the city. Every precinct. Every squad car. The lab guys are already on their way to the car impound to go over that truck from bumper to bumper looking for something to tie it to the hit and run."

"Okay, okay," I say. "I apologize but nevertheless, if you can't or won't go after Biff Claymore, I will. I'll let you know if I learn anything. Meanwhile you might want to think about assigning a little protection to Harvey Senior who is now all that stands between Biff and that ten figure estate the old man's so proud of."

"I thought he had a bodyguard."

"He does. Abe Fallon. And how do we know Abe isn't in on it with Biff?"

"Hey, Joe, tell me. Is there anybody that you DON'T suspect?"

"Cardinal Spellman. See you, Sarge."

I start to walk away. Horvath calls after me,.

"Remember what happened last time you went out on your own, half cocked,"

"I'm not likely to forget, Sarge." I say back over my shoulder just before I walk out.

As I hurry down the precinct stairs, I realize that if I am to talk with Biff Claymore I'm going to have to catch him alone outside of his apartment and that means one thing. Surveillance. Interminably boring surveillance, hanging around his apartment house and waiting for him to appear. My teeth hurt thinking about it but what choice do I have. I check my watch. The time is two-twenty. Jonas said Biff went out a few afternoons a week for the gym but he didn't say what time. Early, late, I have no idea but I'd better get over there fast or risk missing him.

I hop a cab and head for Biff's apartment house on West 48th. There's a parking spot directly opposite the entrance and we pull into it. My cabbie's name is Marco from Puerto Rico and he's a pretty sharp guy. I tell him we may be doing a lot of waiting around this afternoon and he says he doesn't care as long as the meter's running. His face falls a little when I tell him I'm not a private eye and there's no dame involved but he perks up when I mention Stillman's gym. It's dead ahead about nine blocks north on Eighth Avenue, he tells me. He says he once drove Rocky Marciano there from Grand Central Station. A nice guy, he says. Very friendly.

I'm just about to get out of the cab and cross the street to chat with Jonas. No sense sitting here if Biff is already out for the day. But before I can open my door, Biff emerges from the entrance. If he's decided to go to Stillman's he's hardly dressed for it. He's wearing a three piece dark suit with a black tie. His only concession to informality is a woolen driver's cap and it doesn't take me long to figure out why. At that moment a shiny new yellow MG sports car with the top down pulls to the curb. Biff comes around the front of the car as the driver gets out and then holds the door open for him. Biff slips him a bill and gets behind the wheel. No, this afternoon Biff has some place in mind beside Stillman's. As he pulls away from the curb, I tell Marco, "Follow that car!" Just like Chester Morris playing Boston Blackie.

I have gotten lucky. Marco turns out to be an excellent driver whose veins are filled with ice water. Biff has roared away from the curb as sports car drivers are wont to do and now he is racing west on 49th Street toward the Henry Hudson Parkway He flies up the ramp and melds into the northbound traffic with me and Marco hot on his tail about seven car lengths back. I guarantee Marco a big tip if he doesn't lose him and promise to pay the fine if he gets a speeding ticket. Marco checks me out in his rearview mirror to see if I'm serious and when he sees that I am, he grins broadly and stomps on the gas.

We start in and out of traffic lanes, always saying close but not close enough to be observed. Biff may have his failings but behind the wheel of the little MG he knows exactly what he's doing. I begin to understand his obsession with Lime Rock. He may feel he's found the one thing he can do well and is determined to fashion the rest of his life around it. We fly by Grant's Tomb and farther up speed past the entrance ramp to the George Washington Bridge. By the time we reach 233rd Street, we are in the Bronx and this is where Biff exits. We follow discreetly. He turns west and very shortly we are at the corner of 233rd and Webster Avenue where he slows and enters the main gate of the Woodlawn Cemetery and Crematorium. We let him get in deep before we follow. He pulls into the parking lot for the main building and quickly gets out of his car. He checks his watch and then jogs to the front entrance. We pull in and park several spaces down from the MG.

I get out of the cab. First things first. I want a closer look at that little yellow car. Like a lot of sports cars it's adorned with stickers and decals. On the back is a plaque for the SCCA (Sports Car Clubs of America). Off to the side is a decal for MG Car Club, New York. I circle around and find a parking permit affixed to the corner of the windshield. It reads: "Watkins Glen Grand Prix 1954 Preferred Parking." Watkins Glen is a well-known racing venue in upstate New York. In many ways it's what Lime Rock aspires to be. Biff should have removed that sticker months ago but the fact that he hasn't speaks volumes about his obsession with racing and his desperate need to be an important part of the scene.

Obviously Biff's presence here is all about the death of his brother and arrangements for the funeral service and internment. I need to go inside to see what's going on but first, something else needs attending to. I look around to make certain I'm not being observed and then I lift the bonnet and quickly pull a couple of wires loose, disabling the distributor. I close the bonnet and head inside. Woodlawn is a huge place sprawling over 400 acres with well over 200,000 interred on its grounds. It is the final resting place for hundreds of the rich and famous like Fiorello LaGuardia, Herman Melville, Bat Masterson, Joseph Pulitzer, Victor Herbert and F.W. Woolworth, proving that death is the great equalizer. I remember that the papers said Lila Claymore was buried here only a couple of weeks ago. Now she will be joined by her son. I wonder if there is a Claymore family mausoleum. If so I can guarantee it didn't come cheap.

I walk through corridors and up and down staircases until I finally come to a chapel where Harvey Senior and Biff are up by the altar talking in low tones to a somber looking gentleman in a dark suit. Abe Fallon is at the old man's side and looking closely, I see that Fallon has a grip on Claymore's elbow, supporting him. Senior does not look well. He is slightly bent over and his skin has a grayish pallor. I can't hear what's being said but it's obvious two deaths within a month have taken their toll. Suddenly the old man sags and almost falls to the ground. Fallon is able to grab him and hold him up and then sit him down gently into a nearby pew. Biff hurries off and returns in a moment with a small paper cup of water from a drinking fountain. Senior drinks, then nods his head slowly. Fallon helps him to his feet and they start to walk slowly toward the entrance to the chapel. I hurry to get out of sight and a few moments later they are past me and heading for an exit to the parking lot.

From the shadows of the doorway I watch as a limousine pulls up and Fallon helps the old man into the back seat and then climbs in after him. Biff watches solicitously as the door closes and the car starts off toward the exit. A moment later Biff walks over to his sports car and slips behind the wheel.

The key in the ignition produces nothing but an ominous click.

He tries again. Another click. By this time I have walked over to the car and am standing by the passenger door.

"These limeys," I say. "No clue how to build a car".

Biff looks up at me and scowls.

"What do you want?" he snarls.

"A kind word, a smile, a moment of your time."

"Get lost."

"I once was lost but now I'm found," I tell him.

"What?" he says, obviously not a good Protestant churchgoer.

"I'll tell you who's lost, Biff. Ethan Goodbody. Any idea where I can find him."

"What are you talking about?"

"Ethan Goodbody. The guy who ran down your mother in cold blood. The guy who murdered your brother's ex-girlfriend and probably also murdered your brother, all on your behalf."

"Are you crazy?" he says. He tries the key again. Click. He opens his car door and steps out, then moves to the front of the car. I move with him.

"The police already have you at the top of their suspect list. If I were you I'd rat out Ethan and make a deal for yourself before the people of New York schedule you for a seat in their favorite chair."

"Go away, mister. You're annoying me."

"Sorry, these questions have to be asked. I'll try again. Where is Ethan Goodbody hiding out?"

He looks at me angrily and takes several steps in my direction.

"I don't know because I never heard of the guy. Now get out of my sight."

"Or what?"

I'm six-one and in pretty good shape. This little weasel is barely five-eight if that and kind of puny looking. I'm not much worried about his response to 'or what?'.

He steps closer. We're only a foot or so apart. He starts to raise his fists when I am suddenly slugged in the jaw by a ballpeen hammer and I find myself on my ass on the asphalt. Now how the hell did that happen?

"Go away, Mr. Bernardi. Leave me alone."

I struggle to my feet as he walks back to the bonnet and starts to lift it.

"Hey!" I yell. There's plenty of fight left in me. I promise myself I won't be sucker punched again.

As I lumber toward him. he squares off in front of me and starts to throw a punch at my head. Hah. I parry it easily just as a six foot wide tree trunk slams into my solar plexus. I drop my hands protectively and the tree trunk's baby brother lands on my cheekbone and I head for the asphalt again. This is suddenly getting very embarrassing.

As I try to clear my head, a bronze hand reaches down to me.

"Help you up, mister?

I look up. Marco is leaning down to help me. I grab his hand and he hoists me to my feet.

"Hey, Pancho, this is none of your business," Biff says with a racist sneer.

Marco looks at him, properly apologetic.

"Oh, I am so sorry, senor. I do not wish to interfere. Please forgive me." As he says it, he takes out a switchblade knife and flips it open and then starts to casually clean his fingernails. "On the other hand, this gentleman seems to have questions for you. Maybe it would be better if you would answer them." He smiles at Biff who does not smile back but tosses a look of contempt in my direction.

"Your bodyguard?" he asks.

"He'll do for now," I say. "Where's Ethan Goodbody?"

"I told you, I never heard of him."

Marco stops with the fingernails and leans up against the sports car. He take the sharp point of his knife and touches it against the gleaming yellow fender. He smiles at Biff, saying nothing. He doesn't have to.

"No!" Biff gasps.

"Ethan Goodbody," I repeat.

"I swear to God, I don't know him. Tell him to put the knife away."

"Rance Luckett," I say.

Biff quickly nods his head.

"He's got a racing team. He's the one who said he could get me a piece of the Lime Rock deal."

"How'd you meet him?" I ask.

"At Watkins Glen. I was there for the Grand Prix and we kind of ran into each other in the parking lot. He admired my car and one thing led to another. I think I remarked what a great thing Watkins Glen was and it was too bad it wasn't a little closer to New York which was when he told me about the plans for Lime Rock."

"And of course you wanted in."

"Hell, yes, I wanted in. It's gonna be a million dollar operation, Lots of millions more likely."

"Is that when you met Dwayne Tolliver?"

"Dwayne was there. Rance introduced us."

"And Dwayne spelled out how you and your half-million dollars could become a part of the Lime Rock family."

Biff shakes his head violently.

"It wasn't like that. Rance wanted me in but Dwayne said there was no room. The operation was fully subscribed. They didn't want me or need me."

I nod knowingly.

"And what happened a couple of days later?" I ask.

Biff frowns, probably wondering how a guy who looks as dumb as me can actually be pretty sharp.

"Well, yes, something happened. I got lucky. One of their investors had to drop out and Dwayne came to me and asked if I was still interested."

"Sure, he did. And Lucky You told him what?"

"Hell, yes, I was stlll interested. I signed the papers right there and then."

"And the initial fifty thousand dollars?"

"Anselm got it for me."

"Anselm Fosythe III. Your lawyer."

"That's right."

"And your father knew all about what you were doing?"

"Anselm said he did. Anyway it didn't make any difference. Anselm could sign on the account. Pop arranged it that way in case he got hit by a stroke or a heart attack. Somebody had to be able to get to the money."

I nod again. Good old selfless Anselm, ready to pitch in in a crisis for the good of the firm. What a guy.

"And where's Rance now, Biff?"

"How should I know? Up at Lime Rock I suppose."

I shake my head.

"He's here in the city." I say.

"News to me," Biff says.

"Heard from Dwayne Tolliver lately?"

"Matter of fact, he called me yesterday to let me know how well things were going along."

"Yes, I was up there myself, "I say. "Saw everything first hand."

"Then you know," he says brightly.

"Yes, Biff," I say with a smile. "I know."

I have no more questions for Biff Claymore who I'm beginning to believe is a clueless dupe. However, I now have new avenues that need exploring. Marco puts away his pig sticker and we head for the cab leaving Biff to deal with his disconnected distributor. I wave goodbye to him as we head out of the parking lot toward the street. I turn and look back. Biff has the bonnet open now and he is looking into the engine compartment, scratching his head, hopelessly at sea.

Marco drops me off at the Astor. I hand him a hundred and fifty bucks and thank him profusely for his help. He grins broadly. Tonight he will take his wife and their two little ones out to a fine restaurant in celebration. He drives off as I go inside and head for the desk.

"Bernardi. 844. Any messages?"

The clerk gives me the fisheye.

"Excuse me," I say. "Marty Piletti, 844."

The clerk smiles and reaches in my box.

"Just one, Mr. Piletti," he says as he hands me a small hotel envelope.

I rip it open. The message is short and sweet.

"Urgent. Call me immediately. Horvath."

CHAPTER EIGHTEEN

"We took 'em down about an hour ago," Horvath says. "Got 'em both. They were holed up in a rooming house in Bay Ridge. The landlady's sister is married to a cop and as soon as she heard what the new roomers were like, she told her husband."

"Great work, Sarge," I say. I feel like a huge weight has just been lifted from my back.

"We're sweating Luckett in the back room. He's a tough nut and we're not getting much. I gave him twenty minutes of loving kindness. My partner, Fred Schmidt, is in with him now. Fred's approach to guys like Luckett is a little less gentle."

"What about Goodbody?"

"He's in the prison ward at Belleview hanging on by a thread. He tried to run for it. Came out of the house, firing at anything that moved. He never made it to the sidewalk."

"Keep him alive, Sarge. He knows a helluva lot."

"The doctors say it's fifty-fifty. Meanwhile, we're hoping to get something out of Luckett but so far all we get is bullshit. He doesn't know anything about any murder or any hit and run. As far as he knows somebody stole Goodbody's truck off the street and they were trying to figure out how to get back to Lakeville when the cops busted in and tried to arrest them."

"Innocent as a babe," I say.

"And he has no idea why his pal Ethan resisted arrest."

"Probably has a thing about jailhouse food."

Horvath gets up from his desk.

"Let's go see how Fred's doing."

I follow him down a corridor to a door at the end. We go in. It's cramped and windowless but one wall is a wide view of an interrogation room. It's a window on our side, a mirror on the other. We see in. They don't see out. Rance Luckett is seated at a table, manacled to a U-bolt, while a heavy-set guy in a white shirt and rolled up sleeves is pacing around the table. His tie is yanked halfway down his shirt front and the moisture stains at his armpits tell me it's hot in there. He's obviously uncomfortable and annoyed and makes no secret of it. Luckett is doing his best to stay calm but it isn't easy.

"I'm tellIng you—"

"You're telling me crap, shithead," Schmidt barks at him. "You've been telling me crap for the last fifteen minutes and I'm tired of listening to your bullshit and your bellyaching. " As Schmidt walks behind the seated Luckett he takes his bare hand and swats him hard on the head. "Are you listening to me, asshole?"

"I want my lawyer," Luckett whines.

"You mention that lawyer again and I'm going to bust your nose. You understand me? Now tell me about how you and your buddy ran down Lila Claymore in that red pickup truck."

"I didn't run anybody down. I wasn't there. I don't know what you're talking about," Luckett says.

"Hey, you're not hearing me. We've got the truck. We've been all over it like manure in a tomato patch. You ever hear of fingerprints, dumbo?"

"I never said I wasn't in the truck. I said I didn't know nothin' about any hit and run."

Schmidt swats him again, hard.

"Hey, don't lie to me. You lie to me, cornpone, and what's going on in here now'll seem like pattycake, you understand?" When Luckett doesn't respond Schmidt hits him again. "I said, you understand, dumb fuck?"

"Sure, I get it," Luckett mumbles.

"No, buddy, you don't get it. You haven't got a clue. We have your pal Goodbody for first degree murder, dead bang, eyewitnesses, the whole thing. The only question I got left it whether you get to sit in his lap when he gets the chair or maybe you can convince me you were forced into helping him. Do you hear me? Am I getting through to you? Do you want to walk away from this or do you want that long ride up to Sing Sing where they fry you like a pork chop?"

Luckett looks up at him.

"I want my lawyer," he says again.

"When hell freezes over, pal," Schmidt tells him leaning forward within inches of his face.

In that instant Luckett spits in Schmidt's face. Schmidt instinctively jumps back, then in a fury throws a right cross to Luckett's head. If it didn't break his jaw, he's damned lucky.

Horvath leans over to the glass and taps on it several times. Schmidt looks up and then heads for the door and walks out. Luckett remains manacled in his chair, his head lolling on his chest. A moment later Schmidt enters our little observation room, wiping off his face with a handkerchief.

"A real tough nut, Kay," Schmidt says.

"Kay?" I say.

"The last guy who called me Karol who didn't outrank me is walking patrol in Bed Stuy," Horvath says.

I nod.

"Then I can call you—"

"You can call me Sarge," he says. He turns to Schmidt. "What's this about a lawyer?"

Schmidt shrugs. "Soon as I looked at him sideways, he started whining he wanted his lawyer here. I told him I'd make the call for him."

"Did you?"

"Hell, no. We got these two yoyos for two, maybe three murders. You think I'm going to let some lawyer in here to save their worthless hides?"

"He give you a name?" I ask.

Schmidt looks over at me as if noticing me for the first time. Horvath introduces me as one of the good guys and Schmidt relaxes.

"Gave me a name and a phone number. Tolliver. Dwayne Tolliver."

Horvath and I exchange a look.

"Didn't that Chief of Police in Durham tell you that Tolliver had been disbarred?" I say.

"He said he thought he had, because of the New York felony conviction," Horvath replies.

"We need to check that out," I say.

Horvath nods.

Schmidt checks his watch.

"How much more we gonna give this guy, Kay? Me and a couple of the other boys have a five-thirty meeting at the rectory with the monsignor about next week's church fair."

"Sure, Fred. Take off. I'll have another go at him in a few minutes."

"Nice meeting you," Schmidt says to me as he goes out.

"Come on," Horvath says to me. "Like you said, there's something we have to check on."

We go back to his desk where he places a phone call to the District Attorney's office and asks for Gina LaScala. He looks at me, covering the mouthpiece.

"Assistant D.A. We hung around together before I met my wife. Great gal. Sharp as hell and very very talented." He leaves no doubt as to what he means by that last compliment. A moment later Gina comes in the line and Horvath kids her along for a minute or two before he gets down to business. He needs a big favor and very fast. When he mentions the Claymore name I sense she is suddenly paying closer attention. There's a guy named Dwayne Tolliver. Convicted here in New York about sixteen years for floating bad paper. Fourteen months at Rikers and in the bargain the state supposedly lifted his ticket. Question is, did they or didn't they? Could she take a quick look and get back to him right away? She apparently says she will and Horvath hangs up with a smile on his face.

"38-21-35," he says. "Those were her good numbers. IQ of 151. That's the number that kept getting in the way of a perfectly beautiful relationship. First time I went out with my wife I said to her, 'Baby, what's your IQ?'. She says back to me, 'What the hell's an IQ?' We've been getting along great for over thirteen years now."

The phone on the desk rings. Horvath picks up.

"Ninth Precinct. Sergeant Horvath."

He listens intently and whatever is being said, it's important.

"Uh-huh..... When?.....No, I understand. I'm on my way. Be there in ten minutes." He hangs up. "Caruso!"

A detective at a nearby desk lifts his head.

"Yo, Sarge," he says.

"There's a mutt back there in Room One. Toss him in a cell until I get back."

"You got it."

Horvath starts for the stairway. "Let's go," he says. "Goodbody's awake."

We dash down the stairs and out the door. Horvath's unmarked car is parked at curbside. We climb in and he pulls away leaving rubber on the asphalt. He flips a switch to activate the blinking red dashboard light and the siren and turns onto 1st Avenue, all systems go. It's a straight twenty block shot up from 5th to 26th Street and Horvath is supplementing the siren with loud blasts on the horn. Cars scatter everywhere. Maniac on the loose.

Horvath lied. We make it in nine minutes. We take the elevator to the prison ward located in the fourth floor. When we get off we're immediately confronted by floor to ceiling chain link and two well-armed uniformed officers. They recognize Horvath and open the gate to let us in. Horvath makes a beeline for a doctor who is standing by the admitting desk going over some papers on a clipboard. He looks up as Horvath approaches him, then glances at his watch and nods with an appreciative smile.

"You're prompt," the doctor says.

"Want to catch him before he dies."

He introduces me. The doctor's name is Macklin. He's the resident assigned to the ward. It's my guess he didn't volunteer for this post.

"He's weak," Macklin says. "He's lost a lot of blood. He's got a bullet lodged in his spine and I've had to give him morphine. I can't guarantee that he'll be coherent or that he won't die in the next ten minutes."

"Save the speech Doc," Horvath says. "This is on me. You're off the hook. If there's heat I'll take it."

With me following close behind they go through another security gate and head down a long corridor flanked on both sides by barred rooms each housing a single prisoner-patient. Unlike a prison where the appearance of a stranger leads to a lot of obscene yammering and cat calling, it's deathly still in here. No jailbird gets a free ride into Belleview so in most cases these are people on the way out and they know it. The smell of death is everywhere.

Goodbody is lying flat in his back on a narrow bed. He's hooked up to a couple of monitors and an IV drip is feeding painkiller into his left arm. His eyes are closed but you can see he's alive by his shallow breathing.

Horvath leans in close. I'm right beside him as he does.

"Ethan Goodbody," he says.

Slowly Goodbody opens his eyes and turns his head slightly to look at the detective.

"I'm Detective Sergeant Horvath from the Ninth Precinct."

A humorless smile forms on Goodbody's lips.

"Good for you," he rasps. His voice is barely audible.

"I have questions for you," Horvath says.

"Yeah. Guess you do," Goodbody says quietly.

"We think someone hired you to walk into the police station and shoot Daphne Gennaro."

"Never heard of her," he says. His eyes shift and he looks at me and that faint smile reappears. "Looky here, the junior G Man. You're one lucky sonofabitch, G Man."

"Luckier than you," I tell him.

"Hey, Goodbody, look at me," Horvath says. "You can do yourself some good here by cooperating."

Goodbody starts to laugh but the moment he does, pain shoots through his body and he gasps.

"Some good with who? Old Scratch? Hardly think so. He don't take kindly to negotiatin'."

"You're not dead yet. You got a chance."

"I got squat. You know it. So do I."

"You die now whoever hired you gets away with murder."

"Am I supposed to think that's bad? Go peddle your bullshit someplace else, cop. I'm not buyin'."

"So Biff Claymore walks away scot free."

"Claymore? That stupid little runt? Jesus, man, what the hell do you use for brains?" Suddenly he starts coughing and as he does you can see the excruciating pain swarming through his body. Dr.

Macklin nudges me aside and leans down for a closer look.

"That's enough for now, Sergeant," he says.

"A couple more minutes."

"You're liable to kill him."

"I'll send flowers." Horvath looks down again at Goodbody. The coughing has subsided. "Goodbody, look at me. You're telling me Biff Claymore didn't hire you."

"I'm tellin' you nothin'," Goodbody gasps. "I ain't no polecat. I don't rat on nobody. Now get the hell outta my sight."

"Tolliver," Horvath says. "Was it Dwayne Tolliver?"

Goodbody tries to lift his head. His eyes are filled with rage. "Get outta my sight, you sonofabitch!" he says and then suddenly he spasms and falls back on his pillow and his eyes close and his head lolls to one side.

Macklin shoves me out of the way and leans in close. He puts his fingers on Goodbody's carotids, then uses his stethoscope to listen for a heartbeat. After a few moments, he straightens up.

"He's gone," he says.

A few minutes later we're standing out by the admittance desk. If Horvath is sorry that Goodbody is dead, he does a good job of covering it up. I think as far as Horvath and a lot of cops are concerned, a dead mutt makes the world a better place. Even better they haven't yet met the lawyer who can help a dead perp weasel his way out of a pine box.

The phone rings and after answering it, the security officer manning the desk holds out the receiver to Horvath. Horvath takes the call and after a moment I see his face screw up into an expression of confusion. He takes out a pencil and using a pad in the desk, jots down some notes. He speaks in monosyllables and finally hands the phone back. He turns to me, puzzled.

"Gina," he says.

"That was quick," I reply.

"I told you she was smart," Horvath says. "1939. State of New York vs Dwayne Tolliver. Three violations of Section 571 of the penal code. Guilty on all three counts. Sentenced to not less than one nor more than two years at the Rikers Island facility. Additionally defendant is permanently barred from the practice of law in the state id New York."

"Aha," I say.

"That's not all," Horvath says. "Attorney for the defendant. Anselm P. Forsythe III."

Whoa, I think to myself. There's an unexpected bend in the river. But what the hell does it mean? Suddenly all the relationships in this mare's nest are turned topsy turvy.

"It's a new ballgame, Sarge," I say.

"Maybe, maybe not. Right now I'm going back to the station house and unload on Rance Luckett. He needs to know his cohort is dead."

I shake my head in confusion.

"If he knows he's dead, how is that an incentive to talk?" I ask.

"Did you ever hear of a dying declaration, Joe?"

"Enlighten me."

We head for the elevators.

"It's like a deathbed confession only it concerns testimony. The courts have held that if a person is dying and knows that he is dying, anything that he or she might say in such a state is admissible in a court of law as evidence. For example, I draw your attention to Ethan Goodbody's declaration that his boss and good friend Rance Luckett was the one who hired him to kill Daphne Gennaro and also run down and kill Lila Claymore."

"But he never said that."

"Didn't he? I must have a hearing problem. In any case Luckett has no idea what he told me, if anything, and if I work if right, I may have him singing like Patti Page before the night is out. Want

173

to watch?"

I shake my head as we get into the elevator and start back down to the ground floor.

"I think I'll pay a visit to Anselm Forsythe III."

"What for?" Horvath asks. "Goodbody is dead. He's no longer a threat to you or your girlfriend."

"I know that. It's the boy scout in me, Sarge. I'm partial to nice tight knots. I hate loose ends which is what we have here,"

"You're not going to do anything dumb, are you, Joe?" Horvath asks as we cross the lobby of the hospital and head for the main entrance.

"Who, me? I'll be perfectly safe. I'm just going to ask him a few questions. Better yet I may ask them of Harvey Claymore. I'd love to know what the old man saw in Forsythe that prompted him to take him into his business circle."

Horvath heads for his car.

"Can I drop you somewhere?"

I shake my head.

"I'll grab a cab."

"Suit yourself."

I watch as Horvath pulls into traffic and then executes a perfectly illegal U-turn on 1st Avenue and heads back to the station house. I look around for a cab. For the first time I am beginning to see the entire picture and it is very, very ugly.

CHAPTER NINETEEN

It's past seven o'clock and the sun is sinking below what's left of the skyline to the west. The chances of finding Forsythe in his office at this hour are practically nil but I don't know where else to look. He has no home address listed in the Manhattan phone directory which means he either lives outside the city (unlikely) or his phone and home address are unlisted. The cab drops me off at the corner of Seventh and 48th Street. The theater district is dark on Monday evenings and many of the area restaurants go dark as well which means that street and sidewalk traffic are lighter than usual. I hurry to the entrance of the office building and take the elevator to the fourth floor. Dim corridor lamps provide scant illumination at this hour and the hallway is eerie in the extreme. The sound of the silence is deafening as I stride quickly to Suite 422. Farther down the hall I see an open office. Next to the doorway is a cleaning crew trolley. They start early in this building. I know before I knock on Forsythe's door that no one is there but I knock anyway. I try the handle. Locked. What now? It's times like this that I wish I carried a pen knife.

I look down the corridor to the cleaning cart. Okay, I'll take a look. Quickly I hurry toward the open doorway. From inside I can hear the whine of a commercial vacuum cleaner. Cautiously I peer in. A heavy-set woman with her back to me is working on the carpet in the anteroom. I quickly check out the cart and at first I don't find anything I can use. Then I spot the paper bag at the bottom of the cart and from the great aroma emanating from it, I'm pretty sure this is the lady's dinner. I open the bag and check the contents and am rewarded for my nefarious behavior by finding a stainless steel dinner knife. I put the bag back and filch the knife. I'll return it shortly.

I hurry back to Forsythe's office and waggle the knife between the door and the jamb where the lock is located. In the process I'm leaving obvious cuts and scars in the woodwork. Regardless of whether I find anything useful inside, Forsythe will know he had a night visitor. Frankly I don't care. Twice I think I have it and twice the knife slips but on the third try I am able to get the lock sprung and I quickly push open the door and step into the office, closing the door behind me.

The curtains are half drawn so it is not inky black and I can move about without stumbling into the furniture. I open the curtains all the way but it"s a temporary fix. The sun is setting quickly now and soon the light from outside will be gone. I dislike having to turn on a lamp but I have no choice. I start by rifling Forsythe's desk. It's hard going because I don't know exactly what I'm looking for. Best would be some document tying Forsythe to Tolliver or Goodbody or Luckett, something I can bring to the police or, maybe more importantly, to Harvey Senior to prove to him the sort of danger he could be in. My eyes search the room and settle on a dozen filing cabinets lined up against the far wall. I cross over to them and open the L drawer looking for the name Luckett. Nothing. Nor is there a Goodbody under the G's. Under T I find a folder on Dwayne Tolliver but it's old and yellowed and involves the sixteen year old case that got Tolliver disbarred. There are two entire cabinets devoted to Claymore and a quick perusal shows the filed material to be business related. Maybe if I had several hours I could find something but for the moment, I'm stymied.

It's then that I notice the blinking red light coming from a device on Forsythe's desk. I go to inspect it. It bears the name 'Ansafone' and appears to be some sort of answering device for Forsythe's phone. Cheaper than a receptionist, I guess. I examine it carefully. One of the buttons reads 'Play'. I hesitate momentarily, then press it. When I do, Dwayne Tolliver's voice jumps out at me.

"The police have arrested Rance and Ethan. They are good boys and will say nothing to implicate us but we are out of time. What needs to be done must be done right away, Anse, and it must be done by you. Now. Otherwise it's all been for nothing. If you can't do it, we disappear and leave Rance and Ethan to the police."

My gut tightens and I start to shake. It's out in the open now for anyone to see and unless the police get there in time to stop it, Harvey Claymore isn't going to last the evening. I fumble in my wallet for Horvath's card and call the Ninth Precinct. I ask for Horvath and am told he's unavailable. That means he's in back grilling Rance Luckett. I tell the desk sergeant that he has to get a message to Horvath immediately. It's a matter of life and death. He has to send a unit to Harvey Claymore's residence now. Otherwise he'll be looking at another murder.

I hang up and race from the office. By the time I hit the street I'm in a full blown panic. I look around for a cab and see none. I look in every direction and spot the Cort Theater. At this time of night the street should be crowded with cabs filled with theatergoers but no, it's Monday. No show, no cabs. I turn and hurry to the corner of Seventh Avenue. Three cabs fly by, all occupied. A cruiser approaches across the way but before I can hail him, a woman laden down with packages beats me to it. I check my watch. Seven-twenty-nine. I'm about to dash across Seventh to the other side when a cab swoops down on me from behind, blowing his horn as I step off the curb. I jump back, then wave him to a stop when I see he's unoccupied. I dive into the back seat and give him directions. Nine minutes later we are pulling up in front of Harvey Claymore's three story home on the upper East Side. I hand the cabby a twenty and exit the cab, ignoring my change, then dash up the steps to the ornate front door. I don't see a police car and that bothers me. I push the doorbell and then for good measure, slam the brass door knocker a half-dozen times. For a few moments I think—no, I pray—that no one is home and then immediately I worry that I am too late. I slam at the knocker again loud enough to rattle the good china. Just then the door opens and Abe Fallon glares down at me.

"Are the police here?" I ask him, knowing they are not.

"What do you want?" Fallon asks.

"Where's Mr. Claymore?"

"Upstairs in his bedroom. What do you want?"

I dart past him into the foyer before he has a chance to react.

"Is he alone?" I ask.

"No, Mr. Forsythe is with him. They're talking business."

"God damn it!" I shout in frustration as I turn and run toward the horseshoe shaped staircase that leads to the second floor.

"Hey!" Fallon yells as he starts to follow me.

I'm no racehorse but neither is Fallon and I'm way ahead of him as I hit the second floor. I look in both directions. To my right I see double oak doors and I gamble this is where I will find the old man. I race to them, grasp the handle and throw them open.

Harvey Claymore Sr. is lying in his bed, head propped up by several pillows, eyes closed. Sitting on the bed and hovering over him is Anselm Forsythe III, an ugly looking hypodermic needle in his right hand. He looks back at me in surprise as I shout at him. Quickly he backs away from the bed, fear reflected in his eyes as I charge him. He drops the needle and tries to evade me just as Fallon hurries into the room behind me. The big man takes it all in. The hypo needle, the fear in Forsythe's eyes, his desperate attempt to escape. Forsythe runs toward the bedroom doors. I grab for his sleeve but miss. Fallon doesn't. He blocks Forsythe and then grabs him around the neck. He twists the lawyer's arm behind him and starts out of the room, shoving Forsythe in front of him. Forsythe is screaming now but there's no one around to hear him. I hurry out of the room and watch as Fallon half-drags Forsythe to the staircase landing. Then in one swift move, he picks up Forsythe and holds him high above his head. Forsythe screams. He is stlll screaming as Fallon tosses him down the staircase as if he were throwing out the weekend garbage. Forsythe hits the marble landing and lies there inert, a crumpled mass of flesh. I can see blood starting to seep out of his ear. I'm pretty sure some lawyer somewhere has just lost a potential client.

Fallon looks over at me, neither concerned nor threatening. At that moment someone at the door raps loudly with the brass knocker. The police are on the scene. I meet Fallon's look.

"He slipped and fell," I say. "An unfortunate accident."

Fallon nods and then starts down the steps to get the door.

Within an hour the place is crawling with cops including Horvath who admitted that he had been getting nowhere with Rance Luckett. The phony story about a dying declaration had fallen on deaf ears. I've decided that good old boys like Rance may look slow and sound slow but their thought processes are as sharp as a cottonmouth's fangs. After I explain to Horvath about the message on Forsythe's answering machine, he issues an APB for Tolliver's capture. Later this evening he will go to Forsythe's office and confiscate the machine. If Luckett was not persuaded to talk by the nonexistent dying declaration, he might be very willing to save his own hide after listening to Dwayne Tolliver rat him out on a telephone call.

The medical examiner is on hand. His report will be based on an autopsy conducted at the morgue but his preliminary finding puts cause of death as a broken neck suffered as a result of a fall down the staircase. He has also examined the hypodermic needle and informed Horvath that the syringe was loaded with digitalis. This is a drug used to help heart patients but if taken or injected in a massive amount can cause death by severe digitalis toxicity, usually difficult to detect in an autopsy of a corpse with heart disease.

Fallon and I are questioned separately. Our stories mesh. Forsythe was running toward the top of the stairs when he slipped and fell, tumbling down 28 steps to the marble foyer below. As soon as the police photographer has finished chronicling the man's demise, Forsythe will be loaded into the meatwagon waiting outside and transported to the morgue. Since he has no known relatives, he will eventually end up in an unmarked grave in the city's Potter's Field cemetery on Hart Island. The high and the mighty, the poorest of the poor, all come to the same quiet and permanent end.

It's two hours later. I am alone in the cramped observation room watching as Horvath makes yet another try at Rance Luckett. He has just played him the recorded message from Forsythe's telephone answering machine which Horvath liberated from Forsythe's office without benefit of warrant. Horvath doesn't care since Forsythe is never coming to trial.

He turns the machine off.

"Well?" he says to Luckett who is staring off into space, a cold look on his face. Luckett doesn't respond. "I can't believe you are that stupid, Mr. Luckett. Your close buddy is dead and the only one going to trial will be you and let me tell you about juries, Mr. Luckett. They don't like murder and they are going to want to string somebody up real high and watch him twist in the wind and at the moment, that guy is you. I can't believe you are willing to take this fall on your own which is apparently what your slimy confederate, Dwayne Tolliver, would like you to do. Or maybe I'm wrong.

Maybe you're the brains of the outfit. Maybe you're the one who gave the orders to kill two, maybe three people. Maybe Tolliver was just an innocent bystander. Yeah, I can see him now at your trial, sitting up there in the witness box, innocent as Bo Peep and you know something, who's to say he isn't?"

Finally, Luckett looks back at Horvath.

"I didn't kill nobody," he says.

"I never said you did."

"Your partner said—"

"Forget my partner, this is just you and me now."

"If I tell you the truth, the God's honest truth, I want me a deal. I ain't goin' to no Yankee prison."

"I can't promise you that," Horvath says. "I can promise that if you cooperate it'll mean a lot. Might even be possible to get you a light sentence in a North Carolina prison. All depends on what you know and what you'll swear to."

Luckett thinks about it for a few moments and then nods.

"All right," he says, "I'll tell you how it was."

Horvath gets up.

"Hold that thought," he says as he moves out of the room. In a moment he returns carrying a wire recorder and a microphone which he places on the table.

"I'm going to record your statement, Mr.Luckett. It's for your protection as well as mine. If we say you said something you didn't, you can always point to the tape."

Luckett nods and Horvath turns on the recorder. He speaks directly into the mike.

"My name is Karol Horvath, Detective Sergeant Second Grade, Shield 956. It is 10:51 on the evening of September 20. I am interrogating Rance Luckett in connection with the shooting death of Daphne Gennaro, case number FD-231567, and related subjects. Mr Luckett, have I or anyone else threatened or coerced you into making this statement?"

"No, sir, you have not," he says.

"Very well, you may proceed. Start at the beginning."

Horvath pushes the mike in front of Luckett's face.

He starts off haltingly, embarrassed by the seedy nature of the events but before long he is deeply into it and supplying detail after detail.

As I had surmised the whole Lime Rock thing was a scam from the beginning, cooked up by Tolliver and Forsythe who had kept in touch over the years. It was a simple con. Place an option on some land, lease a few bulldozers, paint a few signs, print some brochures and go in search of wealthy race car nuts with more money than brains. It is a very exclusive operation, so goes the flim flam, with only a fortunate few allowed to participate. A half-million dollars was the buy in. Only six partners were needed. They found one in Dayton, Ohio, and a second in Bar Harbor, Maine. If they had found a dozen like them they all would have been welcomed with open arms. Reel 'em in, get the money, string along the early birds while new suckers were being taken in and at the right moment, disappear.

Biff Claymore was to be the prize. His world was fast cars and he knew little else. Forsythe had his confidence through years of nurturing, assuming the role of understanding father that Harvey Senior never was. The Claymore holdings were worth well in excess of fifteen million dollars and only three people stood in the way of Biff Claymore inheriting it all. It turned out to be four when Daphne Gennaro notified Harvey Junior that she was carrying his child. But then, what's another murder when two are already on the drawing board?

Luckett was chosen to meet and woo Biff at the Watkins Glen championship meet in July. It was absurdly easy to get him involved. The only issue was an initial fifty-thousand which Forsythe was able to supply using company funds. Then came the problem of the balance. Four hundred and fifty thousand was too much for Forsythe to siphon off on his own. Too many of the wrong kind of questions would be asked. If only I had the power, Biff, there's nothing I would deny you, Forsythe told him, further welding his relationship, knowing full well that when Biff inherited the company, he would leave the day to day operation in Forsythe's hands. Fifteen million dollars just waiting to be looted.

"And Goodbody?" Horvath asks him.

"Hiring Ethan to do the dirty work was a no brainer. Ethan was a man who liked to hurt people and had no compunctions about killing if it came to that. The mother was easy, slow moving, walking with a cane. Ethan had slammed into her and rolled over her inert body with never a second thought. She was almost too easy and Ethan was looking for something to get his juices going.

"Then came the girl who got arrested with her friend for soliciting and tossed in a holding cell in the back of the Ninth Precinct. She used her one phone call to call Harvey, the son. He told her he'd come and get her out but instead he called Forsythe who was at the old man's place playing bridge with the company appraiser and his wife. Forsythe told the kid he'd take care of getting her released but when he hung up, he phoned Ethan and told him where to find the girl. Now Ethan gets excited. This is the kind of challenge he's been looking for. Blowing the girl away while she's in a cell in a police precinct, that takes balls, and Ethan was always eager to prove how big his really were."

" And the uniform? Where'd that ciome frim?" Horvath asks.

"Hey, didn't I just finish tellin' you Ethan had balls? He goes over to Greenwich Village, looks around for a cop about his size, waits his chance, then jumps him and beats the crap out of him, takes his uniform and tosses the guy into a garbage dumpster. He's in there ten hours and half dead when they finally find him."

"So he kills young Harvey's girlfriend but when his gun jams he's got a problem because the other woman can identify him," Horvath says.

"Right but Ethan's not worried. He figures he'll catch up with her in a day or two but then the boy scout sticks his nose into it and he gets himself shot at the hotel."

"And you take him to a doctor."

"I sure wasn't going to let him bleed to death. Anyway after that Ethan, he figures the boy scout has the dame stashed somewhere so he needs to rattle his cage to make him give her up. Where is he? Who knows? And then the jerk shows up in Lakeville pretending to be an investor. Guy must think he's Dick Tracy or something. A real stupe."

I listen to this with equanimity. Perhaps I was operating a little beyond what good sense would dictate but in the end the two stupes are the stiff back at the hospital and the guy who's cuffed to a table on the other side of the glass singing like Guy Mitchell.

"And Harvey Junior? The so-called suicide?" Horvath asks.

"Ethan. Who else? He catches the guy working at the empty offices, clips him on the chin and knocks him cold. Ethan picks him up, takes him to the balcony and heaves him overboard. Then Ethan finds a piece of paper and writes a two-word suicide note in a 5 year old's scrawl."

"What about Dwayne Tolliver? Where does he fit in?" Horvath asks.

Luckett laughs, genuinely amused.

"Fit in, Sergeant? You ain't been listenin'. Tolliver is it, the brains, the front man, the guy who put it all together. He optioned the land, leased the bulldozers, booked the hotel space, printed the brochures, sweet-talked the suckers and when the time came he gave the orders to kill. We all took orders. Me, Ethan, Forsythe. He promised we'd walk away with millions and we believed him and now? Well, now, Sergeant, you'll be damned lucky if you ever see him again."

And even as Luckett says it, I know he's probably right. Tolliver is one of those people who skate through life leaving behind corpses and shattered lives and with one exception. never paying the price for his actions. Do I care? Not really. Ethan Goodbody is dead and the threat to Bunny is dead with him. That's all that has ever mattered. Tonight I will sleep easily and tomorrow I will take a ride out to White Plains. I desperately want to see Bunny again and take her in my arms and tell her that she is safe and that all is right with the world.

CHAPTER TWENTY

The cabbie who is driving me to White Plains is no Marco but he's a pleasant enough kid from Texas who's working on his PhD in American Lit at Columbia by night and paying the bills by hacking during the day. His name is Terry and he left Austin two and a half years ago. He wishes now he was back there. His high school sweetheart, to whom he's been engaged for seven years, remains in Brownsville, awaiting his return, ever faithful. Or at least he's pretty sure she's been faithful. He knows that HE has, if you don't count hookers. We get into a philosophical discussion about love, what it is, and how you are supposed to know it when you see it. He claims to still be in love with his Amy Sue but confesses it's getting harder and harder to remember what she looks like. He wonders if maybe this isn't a bad sign. He has asked this of a man who has seen and talked to the supposed love of his life maybe three times in the past five years. Unlike Terry I am not riddled with doubts,.

Our conversation is cut short as he turns into the parking lot of the Smith-Lerner Hospital. I spotted a diner a few blocks back and I tell him I'm going to be at least an hour, maybe two, and if he wants to grab a bite, be back by—I glance at my watch—by noon. I exit the cab and watch as he drives off. I go inside in search of Bunny.

I run into Dr. Anders in the lobby and she gives me a glowing report of Bunny's progress. She also warns me that much of the apparent progress is not deep rooted. This is a 60 day program for good reason. Her files include more than a few patients who, feeling hugely better, left after a couple of weeks and were backsliding within days. I tell her I understand. The only thing that matters to me is Bunny's welfare. She tells me I can find Bunny out back on the rear patio. No, she hasn't told her I'm coming. I'm a surprise.

She's sitting on an Appalachian chair at the far end of the patio, a book in her lap. She doesn't notice me until I'm a few feet away. She looks up curiously and then her face breaks into a huge smile as she jumps to her feet and comes to me, arms extended wide. I clasp her to me and she returns my embrace. We stand like that for what seems an eternity. I kiss her atop her head and step back, tossing her my biggest smile.

"You look more beautiful every time I see you," i say.

"You just want to get into my pants," she says.

"That, too."

"This place has rules," she says.

"Then this place sucks. What's the penalty for kissing in public?"

"No dessert for dinner."

"I'll risk it."

I pull her toward me and kiss her lovingly. I feel her respond and her arms are around me, holding me close. I don't want this moment to end but it does and when we separate, I look into her eyes. They are clear and bright and all I can see is the Bunny of yesteryear.

"Can you stand some good news?" I ask her. Her expression changes. Wary but hopeful. "It's over," I say. The relief in her body is visible. Her shoulders sag and she lets out a deep breath.

"In jail?"

"Dead."

"My God," she says quietly. I see tears starting to brim up and

I can only imagine what she's been going through the past few days, reliving that nightmarish moment in the jail cell and then not knowing if the man with the gun would be walking through a door when she least expected it. I fold her in my arms again. Her heart is beating furiously. I can't see her face but I'm pretty sure she's fighting back those tears.

"You, Joe? Was it you?" she asks quietly.

"No, he tried to shoot it out with the police. I wasn't even there."

"Good. I was so worried, Joe. Scared that something would happen to you."

I force a laugh.

"And what could possibly happen to me? Sergeant Horvath and his people did all the work. I just stood around asking dumb questions and getting in the way." I'm not going to tell her about Lime Rock. What would be the point? It's over and done with. She has too much else to deal with than to dwell on might-have-beens involving me.

"Can you stay for lunch?" she asks. "I'm sure I can arrange it."

"I can't, Bunny. I have a job I've been neglecting. I need to get busy."

"Well, sit down then," she says, "and I'll get us some coffee."

"No. No coffee. Let's take a walk. Do they let you stroll around the grounds?"

"Sure. I do it every day."

"Let's go then," I say, taking her hand and leading her onto the gravel path that wends its way around the lawn and gardens of the hospital. We walk along hand in hand like high school sweethearts and she chatters gaily about the gardens spotted here and there around the grounds. It's one of her jobs, she says, weeding and watering the various plants and flowers. Everybody here has at least one job. It's part of the regimen.

"You know, last week when Ginger phoned me, I almost didn't

come." I say it offhandedly and glance over at her to see her reaction. She's frowning as she looks at me. "After all, Bunny, you called Ginger, not me. I wasn't sure you ever wanted to see me again."

"Oh, Joe, how could you think that?" she asks. "I didn't want to. It had been so long, Bunny. You on the road going from town to town. Once in a while a late night telephone call and then another few months of silence. What was I supposed to think? I just didn't want to show up where I wasn't welcome."

She stops and forces me to look at her.

"You will always be welcome in my heart, Joe. Now. In the future. There's never been anyone but you, not really."

I nod. I want to tell her that I understand but in truth I don't. There are so many things I don't understand, so many questions for which I have no answers.

"Why did you leave me?" I say.

There it is. Out in the open. Time for her to give me the answer to the question that has been haunting me for five years.

She looks into my eyes and then she turns away. She's feeling pain and I can see it's crippling her. She wants to speak but she can't. There's a bench nearby. She goes to it and sits. I follow her over and stare down at her. I don't want to be cruel and I don't want to hurt her but this is a question that must be answered and I will not let it slide by.

"Why did you leave me?" I ask again.

"It's complicated," she says.

"Uncomplicate it. I can figure it out."

She won't look at me. What the hell is she so afraid of?

"Ginger said you left me because you loved me," I say.

"It's true, Joe."

"She also told me that if we got married you couldn't give me a child."

Her head snaps up and she looks at me with an expression akin to terror.

"She told you."

"She didn't tell me anything, Bunny. She said if I wanted the truth I'd have to ask you. Well, now I'm asking. I think I have a right to know."

She looks away.

"Yes," she says and then she looks up at me. "Yes, you do have that right and I will tell you. You'll probably hate me for it but I guess it has to come out."

"I could never hate you," I say.

A wry smile crosses her lips.

"Listen first. Then tell me that."

I sit down next to her and try to take her hand. She pulls it away as she stares off into space.

"I was fifteen. His name was Bucky Trumbull. We were in love or at least I was. It was summer. He was eighteen, headed for Dartmouth in September. I wanted to hold onto him forever and I gave myself to him eagerly. We would go east together, find a little apartment near the campus. Life would be good. And then I discovered I was pregnant. He was furious. He screamed at me and walked away and before I knew it, he was gone. No goodbye. Just gone. I didn't know what to do. I couldn't tell my parents. I had no money for a doctor to fix things even if I knew where to find one. I went back to school, not showing but scared to death. One of the older girls had gotten herself into my kind of trouble and she told us how she had used a coat hanger to get rid of the problem. I worked up the nerve to talk to her and she told me how it was done. That night I went into the bathroom and locked the door and did what I had to do."

Her voice is failing her now and tears are starting to run down her cheeks. I take her hand and this time I won't let her pull away. I squeeze her hand tight. Still she will not look at me.

"I started to bleed and then I bled more heavily. The pain was excruciating. I remember screaming and slumping to the floor, then my father coming to the bathroom door and calling out my name. I tried to get up. I couldn't. And then he broke the door down and when he saw what had happened he scooped me up in his arms and he and my Mom drove me to the hospital. The doctors stopped the bleeding. They also told me I'd done a lot of damage to myself and that I would never again be able to conceive."

I put my arm around her and I pull her close to me. Now she is crying in earnest.

"You wanted a big family so badly, Joe, and I knew I could never provide ir. I went along for weeks and months refusing to face reality. I couldn't tell you. I know what you would have said, that it wouldn't matter as long as we had each other but that would have been a lie and sooner or later you would have started resenting me. I couldn't deal with that and when my New York chance came, I took it, hoping that you would forget me and praying that I had the strength to forget you."

We sit there quietly for a long time, each of us with our thoughts. I am still holding her close and she is not pulling away.

"My heart aches for you, Bunny," I say finally. "I can only imagine the terror of what you went through. but there is one thing you must understand. Your inability to bear children, it doesn't matter. Not to me. Maybe five years ago it would have been hard to deal with but I'm older now and I like to think a lot smarter. I'll adopt a dozen kids if that's what it takes but I'm not letting you go again."

For a fleeting moment I consider telling her about Jillian and Yvette but decide that's a topic for another day,

"Look at me," I say. She looks up at me, her cheeks stained by rivulets of tears. "I love you now as much as I ever did. Maybe more. And I know you love me. There's nothing we can't overcome if we trust in each other. Please, Bunny. Trust me now. Believe in me. Don't be afraid."

She nods and holds me close. The barrier that threatened to destroy us has been brought down. I'm feeling a sense of joy that I thought had been lost forever.

"Come on, let's walk," I say as I get up. She takes my hand and we resume our stroll through the grounds of the hospital. We don't say much because it's all been said. When we get back to the main building it's nearly noon.

"I'll call you tomorrow," I say.

"Yes, please do," she says. "Don't forget."

"I won't," I say taking her in my arms and kissing her tenderly. She smiles.

"No dessert for you tonight," she says.

"I'll survive," I say, then turn and head for the parking lot where I see Terry standing by the cab. I look back. She hasn't moved. I wave. She waves back. My heart is full and now I am ready to take on 'Marty'.

We make one stop on the way back to the city. I make a couple of phone calls. One is to the production office at the Cameron Hotel to find out where the company is shooting. The guy manning the office tells me the Waverly Ballroom and he gives me the address. I ask if Hecht will be there. I'm told he will be.

The ballroom sequence is the big (i.e. expensive) scene in the movie and I'm a little put off when I climb the staircase to the second floor and walk onto the dance floor. The place is large. I mean, really large but I see only a hundred or so extras to go along with the small combo up on the bandstand. I know the budget's small but this may strain credulity. They're setting up for the next shot so everyone is just hanging around. I look for Harold Hecht and don't see him but I do spot Ernie Borgnine off to the side gabbing with this gangly kid who looks like he's still in high school.

"Hey, Joe!" Ernie has seen me and waves me over. I join him and he gives me a big smile. "Are you back? I heard you had troubles. Everything okay?"

"Everything's great, Ernie, and I'm back and rarin' to go."

"Terrific," he says. "Say hello to Jerry—Sorry, son, I forgot your last name."

"Orbach. Jerry Orbach."

The kid smiles. I introduce myself. We shake. "Jerry lives a few blocks from here. He's going to Northwestern next year to study theater. He's looking for a few pointers."

"Got any hot tips, Mr. Bernardi?" he asks.

I nod solemnly.

"Learn how to survive on two pieces of toast and a cup of tea a day. Develop a hide like a rhinoceros and whatever you do, do not get involved with actresses or other female impersonators."

The kid laughs. I like him already.

A voice on a bullhorn fills the auditorium.

"Atmosphere! Up front!"

"That's me," the kid grins. "Ten bucks and a free lunch. Hey, but I'm in show business, right?" He waves goodbye and hurries toward the bandstand where all the extras are beginning to congregate. I watch him go and then look back at Ernie who's no longer smiling.

"From that expression, I'd say there's something wrong," I say.

Ernie shakes his head.

"Naw. The picture's coming along great. I think Harold's got some problems but he doesn't tell me and I don't ask."

"Well, I'm just the pushy press agent. I'll ask. Any idea where he is?"

"There's a small office over there right in back of the bandstand. He's spending a lot of time on the phone. Probably there now."

"Thanks," I say and head off. I'm wondering how in God's name Harold can be talking on the phone when he's only a matter of feet away from the bandstand. And then I learn two things about movie making on the cheap. For starters the assistant director has gathered all the chatterers and the sitters and the dancers and crowded them into a mob just in front of Joseph LaShelle's camera. All one hundred extras are in the shot. I hear a call for quiet, then the.A.D. calls for action. Up on the stage the members of the combo mime playing their instruments while someone off camera pounds out the beat on a pair of claves.The dancers dance, chatterers chatter and the couples at the tables sit and drink. After about thirty seconds the A.D. yells "Cut ", Delbert Mann yells "Print" and now LaShelle changes the angle of the camera and the A.D. regroups the extras, moving the close-in dancers from the previous angle to the back and vice versa. I can see now that when these sequences are put together the crowd in the ballroom will appear to be well over three or four hundred. Hollywood ingenuity. I'm in awe of it.

I find Hecht in the little office and as Ernie predicted, he's on the phone. His face lights up when he sees me and waves me into the room. I don't get all of the conversation but it has something to do with release dates for the picture and Harold is getting increasingly frustrated, Finally he hangs up as politely as he can and shakes his head.

"To paraphrase a wiser man than I, God must love morons because he has made so many of them. That guy controls eight theaters in southern Ohio and is convinced that no one in their right mind is going to spend good money to see a rehash or a two year old television show." He shakes his head ruefully. " You know, Joe, I'm beginning to think maybe he and the rest of the morons are right."

"They're wrong and you know it, Harold. You've got a gem in progress here and part of my job description is to make sure everyone involved with this picture maintains a high level of enthusiasm."

"I'm not sure that's why we hired you," Hecht says.

"I am," I say. "On the way here I called an old friend, Mark Goodson, and talked to him about getting Ernie on 'I've Got a

Secret'. He jumped at it. We're penciled in for next week's show."
Hecht beams.

"That was fast."

"Not only fast but good, Harold. By the time I get done everybody in America is going to want to see this picture."

"Yeah," Harold says acidly, "and if we can book a few theaters they may even have a place to go watch it."

"That bad?"

"Not good. Summer's out because we can't compete with the kiddie blockbusters which means a decent date in the spring. Trouble is, everybody has the same idea. 'East of Eden' is already set for March 9. 'Seven Year Itch' is looking at late May. Ernie versus Marilyn Monroe. There's a fair fight for you. 'Mister Roberts' is looking at May or June. 'To Catch a Thief' is gearing up. So is 'Picnic' and 'Guys and Dolls'. Cary Grant, Holden, Brando. Jesus. Blackboard Jungle' is all set for the date I really want. March 19. Gang violence and rock and roll. Whoopie."

"Not your audience," I say.

"No, but if they keep picking off the available theaters, my audience is out in the cold."

I nod thoughtfully.

"So all we have to do is convince these theater owners that Marty is a can't miss, don't miss picture they can't afford to ignore."

"Well said," Hecht responds.

"I'll mull it over," I tell him.

"Good," Hecht smiles. "Don't mull too long. My youngest son says I'm losing my hair over this picture and I'm not big on turning bald."

CHAPTER TWENTY ONE

For the past seven weeks I've been commuting between Los Angles and New York. Harold Hecht and I have been in contact every day and we have gotten lots of favorable press for the stars of our picture and for writer Paddy Chayefsky but even though it isn't stated overtly, I know that there are skeptical reservations about the picture itself, a two year old black and white kitchen sink television drama revisited. I chat with columnists and critics from all over and as I look in their eyes, I can read their minds. It's a television show, for Christ's sake. It was heartwarming and delightful but at its core, it's a little story about little people. It isn't a movie. 'From Here to Eternity' was a movie. 'On the Waterfront' was a movie. 'Marty' is not a movie. The date is November 10th, Veteran's Day. Principal photography is finished and the company is well into post production. Hecht tells me the first rough cut is terrific. Ernie is terrific. Betsy is terrific. Everybody is terrific except for the bird brained theater owners who are still reluctant to book the picture despite the publicity blitz we've mounted over the past couple of months. If I weren't such a calm and mellow fellow, I would have murdered the lot of them weeks ago. As it is the sum total of my frustration adds up to two broken lamps, one shattered mirror, and two traffic tickets. One of the few bright spots in my life is the apprehension of Dwayne Tolliver who was arrested in Vermont trying to sneak across the border into Canada, leaving behind mountains of unpaid bills and a dozen or more angry creditors and irate investors.

It is seven-thirty on Thursday evening and I have just gotten off the plane at LaGuardia airport. I have a reservation at the Astor. On Saturday, Bunny's sixty-day rehabilitation program ends and If I am lucky, I am going to take her home with me. By the time I get to the hotel it will be too late to call her. They shut down early at Smith-Lerner. Ben Franklin and his early to rise philosophy would approve. So I'll go see her tomorrow after I traipse over to Harold's rented facilities where post production remains underway. I have an idea. It's heretical but drastic times call for drastic gambles.

On Friday morning. I walk into Harold's office a few minutes before ten. He gives me a smile and waves me to a seat. His girl brings me coffee and in a lull between phone calls he tells me how happy he is with everything I've done. Great ink, he calls it.

I smile and regard him with forced amusement,

"The operation was a huge success, the doctor said, but the patient died."

Hecht nods in agreement,

"Yes, there's that."

"I have an idea that might turn things around. You'll have to trust me."

"I'm listening," Hecht says.

"Can you set up a screening of the rough cut for early this evening, say around six o'clock."

"I could do that," he says. "A screening for who?"

"I can't tell you that," I say. "If I did you'd say no and I wouldn't blame you, but in this case I have a better perspective on things than you do,"

"A film critic?"

"Not exactly," I say in all honesty.

"And you think this person might be the answer to our problem?"

"Yes, I do."

"I never allow outsiders to see rough cuts," Hecht says.

"I know but he knows how to look at one."

"Everyone says that and mostly they don't," Hecht says. And he's right. A rough cut is the first assembly of the picture. There is no music, many missing sound effects, often muffled dialogue not yet dubbed for clarity, the film exposures are uneven and the transitions between scenes are non-existent. "You trust this guy?" Hecht asks me. "I do," I say, "and here's the deal. If he ends up saying or writing anything that hurts the picture. I will refund you half the fee that you have paid to our company. I'd refund Bertha's half but she tells me she has car payments and a compulsive love of eating."

Hecht stares at me thoughtfully before he answers.

"All right, Joe. You trust this man and I trust you."

"Thanks, Harold. I'll call you later with the exact time. Nobody is to be here except your editor to run the projector. That's part of the deal."

"Okay. You've got balls, Joe. This friend of yours, he could hurt the picture but he can't kill it. But if this stunt backfires it could give you a black eye in the business for a long time to come."

"I know. And I hope you know that I wouldn't risk my career like this if I didn't believe so deeply about this picture."

Hecht stands up and extends his hand across the desk.

"Good luck, friend," he says.

We shake. Now I know what Julius Caesar felt like when he started to get his feet wet in the Rubicon.

As soon as I leave Harold's offices I make a beeline for a phone booth and after making a half dozen calls, I have everything set up for this evening. Now I hurry out to the street and grab a passing cab. We head for White Plains.

I find Bunny working at a rose garden at the west end of the hospital. She's wearing stained work pants and an old blouse and a bandana is covering her hair. Her face is slightly smudged with dirt. She's kneellng on a rubber work pad and scratching away at the base of a bush with a three tined hand rake and she only notices me when I kneel down beside her and kiss her on the cheek. I have given her a start but she smiles when she sees it's me and plants a big wet one on my lips.

"You're early," she says. "I don't get out until Saturday."

"I know. I had picture business with Harold."

"How's it coming? The theater bookings, I mean."

"Not so hot but I think things will improve."

"Ace publicity man on the job?"

"Something like that," I say. "Can I help? How about if I pull weeds?"

She points. "There are no weeds. I got 'em all yesterday."

"I feel useless."

"Just watch. I'll be through soon and we can have lunch."

I nod.

"Mmm. Thursday. That's corned beef hash day."

"Good memory."

I do my Apache imitation.

"Uhhh. Good memory of bad tasting hash. How about civilized lunch in white man restaurant in village."

She smiles, shaking her head.

"They'll never let me go,"

"You'll never know unless you ask," I say.

So she asks and they say okay and that's why we find ourselves at a quiet little table for two in the local Howard Johnson's being waited on by a cheerful product of Louisiana named Clarisse. Bunny opts for a pot pie. I go for the fried clams. No Howard Johnson's anywhere in America has ever served up a bad dish of fried clams.

"How's the baby?" Bunny asks

"Still teething," I say.

I've told Bunny about Jillian and Yvette. She seemed to take it well but I don't know. I'm a certifiable fool when it comes to reading women. Always have been and the years haven't made me any smarter.

"I doubt Jillian's getting a whole lot of sleep," Bunny says.

I shrug.

"She was hell bent on experiencing motherhood in all its phases. Looks to me like she's getting her wish."

Bunny throws me a disapproving smile.

"You're cruel."

I shrug.

"You reap what you sow," I say cavalierly but in reality I feel sorry for Jill. Even with Bridget's help she's having a tough few weeks. I decide to change the subject before Bunny gets the idea I'm an unfeeling oaf. "What time do you want me to pick you up on Saturday?"

"Oh,I don't know," she says. "Sometime after lunch. I want to say goodbye to a lot of people and Dr. Anders may want to give me a farewell pep talk. I hear that's pretty much standard procedure."

"How about one o'clock?"

"Fine."

I jab at a couple of clams and dip them in tartar sauce, stalling for time. Finally I work up the nerve to speak.

"I thought instead of flying straight through to Los Angeles, we might stop in Las Vegas."

"What for?" Bunny asks. "I'm not much of a gambler."

"There are other things to do in Vegas beside gamble," I say, laying my fork on my plate.

She looks up at me. I see a flash of fear and then concern.

"A little chapel off main street," I say. "A kindly parson. Rented flowers and used wedding rings. 'O Promise Me' piped into the room via speakers. It's not exactly St. Patrick's cathedral but it's just as legal."

"Do you really think that's a good idea?" she asks.

"I do."

She looks down at her plate and absently picks at her pot pie.

"All right. If that's what you want," she says.

"Not exactly a response bubbling over with romantic enthusiasm," I say.

"I'm sorry, Joe. You caught me by surprise, that's all. In two days I'm graduating with honors from an alcohol rehab program. I really haven't given a moment's thought to what comes after except to fly back to L.A. with you and then—what was it you said? After that we'll play it by ear. Are we playing it by ear here, Joe, or have you got things pretty much planned out?"

She's got me there.

"Sorry. I broached the subject clumsily and worse, I may have taken too much for granted."

She smiles and reaches for my hand.

"You mean, do I love you? You know I do. I always have even back in those days right after the war when you were still chasing after your ex-wife and I was nothing more than a good buddy."

"Then what?"

"I don't know. Maybe I'm just being stupid. Maybe all that booze has permanently addled my brain. Maybe I'm just a little scared."

"Of what?"

"I wish I knew."

"Okay, forget it." I try not to sound too disappointed which I am. "I'm in no rush, Bunny. This is your call and I can wait for ages if I have to."

"You won't," she says with a smile. "I think I'm just being an overly cautious scared little bunny rabbit who doesn't know her own mind. Let me sleep on it. We're going to be together, Joe, with or without the license. Just give me a chance to decide what I can be most comfortable with."

She's still holding my hand and now I put my other hand atop hers.

"Whatever you decide is fine with me," I say. "I mean it, Bunny. Don't feel pressured. This is your call. As long as we're together nothing else matters."

She nods and smiles.

Back at the hotel, I spend the rest of the afternoon making phone calls. Jill tells me the tooth thing is abating but I can tell from her voice it's far from over. She sounds tired. She asks when I'm coming back to town and I tell her Sunday. I also tell her I'm bringing Bunny. She seems to take that news well but as I said, I read women as well as I read sanskrit.

I get through to Bertha around five o'clock. She's just returned from lunch with Robert Wagner and she's in a terrific mood. Not that we're going to sign him up, she just likes having lunch with Robert Wagner. It's her one real fantasy and I love her for it,. She is also in a good mood because we have done well by Hecht-Lancaster. Not as well as we might have, I tell her, and explain the problem of securing venues for a spring release. Then I tell her about my plan for wooing the independent theater owners. She chokes on it. She can't believe what I've done. We are going to be crucified. When I tell her that I have promised to refund half our fee if it fails, she almost swallows her dentures. I think I may have made a mistake in letting her in on this before the fact. I reassure her that everything will be fine. My words fall on deaf ears. I hang up before things get out of hand. A few minutes later I am out the door and on my way back to Harold's offices, trying hard to ignore the fact that I am putting my carefully nurtured career into what may be terminal jeopardy.

CHAPTER TWENTY TWO

I pull up to the hospital entrance at exactly five minutes to one. The trip from the Astor has been uneventful. Actually it's been mostly aggravating. My driver is a refugee from Bulgaria who came here after the war to escape the Communists and now he's beginning to think he made a mistake. Maybe the Communists are better, he said. He started to rattle off all the things he hated about the U.S.A. and I finally told him to shut up. He took this as a sign that all Americans are unfeeling elitists. If I'd had the money I would have bought him a ticket back to Sofia. Even at 5% I've overtipped him as I tell him he's no longer needed. If he has to deadhead his way back to Manhattan it won't break my heart. This guy is not going to spoil a perfectly wonderful day.

What is it they say about God having his own special way of dealing with Man's hubris. I am about to discover that, not only is the world not my oyster, it isn't even a pint sized mussel. Dr. Anders is in the lobby waiting for me. I suspect she saw my cab pull up. I can tell by the expression on her face that I am in for bad news. My heart sinks. Jesus, have mercy, I think to myself. Tell me I'm wrong. I'm not.

She leads me over to a sofa off at the far end of the lobby.

"She left about two hours ago, Joe. There was nothing I could say or do to make her stay."

"Why? Did she say why?"

She reaches into her pocket and takes out an envelope.

"She left you a letter."

I take it from her but for the moment I don't open it. I mostly stare at my shoes.

"As soon as you left yesterday, she started making phone calls. A half dozen at least. Maybe more. Early this morning, about seven-thirty or so a Western Union boy came to the door with a telegram. It included money. She hurried upstairs and was down in an hour, all packed. She'd already called for a cab. She handed me that letter and asked me to make sure you got it."

I nod, fingering the envelope, still unwilling to open it.

"I don't know what you two talked about yesterday but it frightened her badly. Oh, I'm sure you didn't mean to do that but people like Bunny, they are fragile in ways that you and I cannot imagine."

"I suggested marriage," I tell her.

Anders nods. "Yes, I thought it might have been that. Obviously she's not ready and rather than say no to your face, she decided to run. I've seen it before. As a recovering alcoholic Bunny has made great strides, Joe, but she will always be an alcoholic even if she stays sober."

"Yes. My first wife—" I let it go unsaid.

"Then you know." I nod. "The best you can hope for now, Joe, is that she maintains contact with you by letter or phone. I truly believe that if she straightens herself out, the first one she will turn to will be you."

"Dr. Anders. Dr. Anders. Second floor nurse's station, please." comes a voice on the loudspeaker.

She stands and then puts her hand on mine. "She's not gone, Joe. Not yet. Merely missing. Good luck."

I look up and thank her and she walks off. I sit quietly for several minutes and then I go over to reception and ask the lady at the desk if she could call a cab for me.

A short time later, we're heading south on White Plains Road getting ready to swing onto the Cross Bronx Expressway when I finally get up the nerve to tear open the envelope. It's not a long letter. Apparently there wasn't a lot to say.

> *Dear Joe,*
>
> *I am so sorry. I hate myself for doing this but honestly, darling, I couldn't risk losing you forever and it might have happened.*
>
> *Please try to understand. I look well and I sound good but I am not a complete woman again, not yet, and I must be whole before I can come back to you. And, Joe, I will come back. I give you my solemn promise. I have called an old friend from the New York days who is working on a newspaper in the Midwest. Never mind which one or where it is. Her name is Jackie Phelps and she's starting me out at the very bottom and forcing me to work my way to the top. With hard work, I'll get there. I know I will. I'll phone you once a week, my sacred honor, but I can't write. Postmarks and all that.*
>
> *Be well, think of me always, remember that I love you and that I always wlll and God willing, we will have a long and happy life together.*
>
> *Your Bunny*

I stare at the letter and then read it again and finally I put it back in its envelope and slip it into my pocket. Maybe Dr, Anders has it right. She's not gone, she's just missing. I can live with it. I have to.

It takes forever but Sunday morning finally comes. My flight out of LaGuardia is at 10:35. I've left a 7:00 call with the switchboard and a breakfast order with room service. It'll be delivered at 7:30.

I shave and shower and dress comfortably for the trip. Cashmere sweater, no jacket, no tie. There's a knock at the door and I open it to admit the waiter with my breakfast trolley. I've ordered big so I can avoid the airline food. I sign the chit including a grossly large tip. Bertha will be annoyed but after a good night's sleep I am feeling more optimistic about the situation. I'm taking Bunny at her word and that means sooner or later we're going to be together again and there's no way I can be upset by that possibility.

My eye falls on the Sunday Herald Tribune which was delivered along with breakfast. I pick it up. No, not possible, I say to myself. It's much too soon. But even as I think it, I sort through the sections until I come to Entertainment and the Arts.

And there it is, taking up the entire page. A photo of Ernie and Betsy at the ballroom. A shot of Paddy at his typewriter and another of Ernie and Joe Mantell just hanging out. I look at the headline of the article. "An American Treasure" by John Crosby.

By and large, it's my job to take eager, talented young writers and directors and producers and performers and tell them as gently as I can why they are failing at their chosen profession. You regular readers will know I am exaggerating but the truth is, a lot of what I have to do leaves a sour taste in my mouth. I don't want to be in the business of destroying egos or killing careers but it's my job and, more than that, my responsibility to warn my public when amateurs are lurking about, set on stealing your time and money with an inferior product. I'm not happy about it but I do it. As I said, it's my job.

But then there are days when suddenly, when I least expect it, I am overwhelmed by the euphoria that comes only too seldom when I am treated to a work that reaches deep into my core. I had such a day this past Friday evening. Some of you have probably heard that they are making a motion picture version of the television drama, 'Marty' and like me, you probably asked yourself why.

The original was wonderful. Why do it again, especially if you are going to gunk it up with Hollywood glitter and razzamatazz? Cary Grant as Marty? Monroe as Clara. Move it from the Bronx to Newport, Rhode Island. Sorry, I don't want to see that picture. Well, I'm happy to report that I won't have to and neither will you. Friday evening I spent a magical evening in a cramped projection room with Ernest Borgnine and Betsy Blair and a cast of relative unknowns who took the original 'Marty' and kicked it up several notches. The original was brilliant, the movie version is even more so. The print I watched had no music, no sound effects and occasional dialog I couldn't even hear and still, I was mesmerized. Toward the end I felt my eyes start to moisten and I'm a tough old cookie. I don't do that. But I did.

It goes on like that for another twenty or thirty paragraphs. Ernest Borgnine is a revelation, soft and warm and eminently likable. Betsy Blair, often dismissed as a so-so actress, comes out of her cocoon to break your heart. The new scenes by Paddy Chayefsky don't detract from the story, they flesh it out. If I could have written this piece and put John's name on it, this is what I would have written. My egotistical moment of self congratulation is interrupted by the ringing of my phone. I pick up.

"Joe, it's Harold. My God, man, I can't believe it."

"Me either, Harold. More than I expected."

"Really wonderful, Joe. I heard from Ernie first thing this morning. He's ecstatic. As soon as it's a decent hour on the west coast I'll put a call in to Burt. I know he'll want to congratulate you personally."

"Not necessary, Harold. All I did was beat the drum. You guys made the picture."

"Save that self effacing crap for your memoirs, Joe. As of this moment, I am hiring you and Bertha for every Hecht-Lancaster picture we produce."

"I couldn't be happier. Bertha will do cartwheels."

"And Joe, just for your information. You remember that theater owner in southern Ohio, the one with the eight theaters? He called me a half hour ago and promised me all eight theaters. Any date I want."

For a moment I'm speechless. Harold and I have come a long way to get to this point and I'm feeling pretty proud of both of us. It seems the little picture that couldn't actually can. And it will.

THE END

AUTHOR'S NOTE

'Marty' opened nationwide on April 11, 1955. By the time it ran its course, it had grossed well over $3,000,000 on a budget of $343,000. Critics were universal in their praise.At the Cannes Film Festival it won the prestigious Palme d'Or and following that was tapped by the motion picture academy as Best Picture of the Year. It was one of only two films to be so honored, the other being 'The Lost Weekend'. The film received seven Oscar nominations and swept most of the major awards. Besides Best Picture, it was honored for Best Actor (Borgnine), Best Director (Mann) and Best Adapted Screenplay (Chayefsky). Since this is a work of fiction most of the ups and downs of the movies distribution travails have been invented. Obviously also invented is any and all dialogue involving real life persons. As always the author has nothing but the greatest respect for the celebrities who are part of this work and there has been no intention to demean or denigrate any of them. As for Joe's problems with the Lime Rock crowd, this is total fabrication. There was no Terranova Corporation and no swindle involved in Lime Rock's beginnings. In reality the land was owned by the Vaill family and Jim Vaill, the son, working with John Fitch and the Cornell Aeronautical Labs, was instrumental in creating the race course. Work started in 1955 and the circuit was open for racing in 1957. Today Lime Rock is among the premier racing sites in the country and host course for a wide range of SCCA race meets. And, oh yes, for those of you who loved and admired him (as I did) Jerry Orbach was actually a teenage extra in the sequences at the Waverly Ballroom.

MISSING SOMETHING?

The first nine books in the Hollywood Murder Mystery series are now available from your local bookstore. If not in stock, copies of all nine volumes can be ordered. Barring that, copies are available direct from Grove Point Press. All copies will be personally signed and dated by the author. If you purchase ANY THREE for $29.85, you automatically become a member of "the club". This means that you will be able to buy any and all volumes in any quantity at the $9.95 price, a savings of $3.00 over the regular cover price of $12.95. This offer is confined to direct purchases from The Grove Point Press and does not apply to other on-line sites which may carry the series.

Book One—1947
JEZEBEL IN BLUE SATIN

WWII is over and Joe Bernardi has just returned home after three years as a war correspondent in Europe. Married in the heat of passion three weeks before he shipped out, he has come home to find his wife Lydia a complete stranger. It's not long before Lydia is off to Reno for a quickie divorce which Joe won't accept. Meanwhile he's been hired as a publicist by third rate movie studio, Continental Pictures. One night he enters a darkened sound stage only to discover the dead body of ambitious, would-be actress Maggie Baumann. When the police investigate, they immediately zero in on Joe as the perp. Short on evidence they attempt to frame him and almost succeed. Who really killed Maggie? Was it the over-the-hill actress trying for a comeback? Or the talentless director with 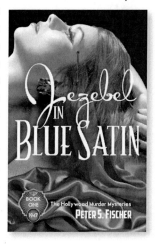 delusions of grandeur? Or maybe it was the hapless leading man whose career is headed nowhere now that the "real stars" are coming back from the war. There is no shortage of suspects as the story speeds along to its exciting and unexpected conclusion.

$12.95 (9.95 to Club Members)

Book Two—1948
WE DON'T NEED NO STINKING BADGES

Joe Bernardi is the new guy in Warner Brothers' Press Department so it's no surprise when Joe is given the unenviable task of flying to Tampico, Mexico, to bail Humphrey Bogart out of jail without the world learning about it. When he arrives he discovers that Bogie isn't the problem. So-called accidents are occurring daily on the set, slowing down the filming of "The Treasure of the Sierra Madre" and putting tempers on edge. Everyone knows who's behind the sabotage. It's the local Jefe who has a finger in every illegal pie. But suddenly the intrigue widens and the murder of one of the actors throws the company into turmoil. Day by day, Joe finds himself drawn into a dangerous web of deceit, dupliciity and blackmail that nearly costs him his life.

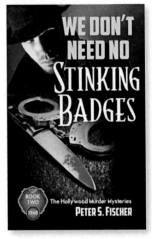

$12.95 (9.95 to Club Members)

Book Three—1949
LOVE HAS NOTHING TO DO WITH IT

Joe Bernardi's ex-wife Lydia is in big, big trouble. On a Sunday evening around midnight she is seen running from the plush offices of her one- time lover, Tyler Banks. She disappears into the night leaving Banks behind, dead on the carpet with a bullet in his head. Convinced that she is innocent, Joe enlists the help of his pal, lawyer Ray Giordano, and bail bondsman Mick Clausen, to prove Lydia's innocence, even as his assignment to publicize Jimmy Cagney's comeback movie for Warner's threatens to take up all of his time. Who really pulled the trigger that night? Was it the millionaire whose influence reached into City Hall? Or the not so grieving widow finally freed from a loveless marriage. Maybe it was the partner who wanted the business all to himself as  well as the new widow. And what about the mysterious envelope, the one that disappeared and everyone claims never existed? Is it the key to the killer's identity and what is the secret that has been kept hidden for the past forty years?

$12.95 (9.95 to Club Members)

Book Four—1950
EVERYBODY WANTS AN OSCAR

After six long years Joe Bernardi's novel is at last finished and has been shipped to a publisher. But even as he awaits news, fingers crossed for luck, things are heating up at the studio. Soon production will begin on Tennessee Williams' "The Glass Menagerie" and Jane Wyman has her sights set on a second consecutive Academy Award. Jack Warner has just signed Gertrude Lawrence for the pivotal role of Amanda and is positive that the Oscar will go to Gertie. And meanwhile Eleanor Parker, who has gotten rave reviews for a prison picture called "Caged" is sure that 1950 is her year to take home the trophy. Faced with three very talented ladies all vying for his best efforts, Joe is resigned to performing a monumental juggling act. Thank God he has nothing else  to worry about or at least that was the case until his agent informed him that a screenplay is floating around Hollywood that is a dead ringer for his newly completed novel. Will the ladies be forced to take a back seat as Joe goes after the thief that has stolen his work, his good name and six years of his life?

$12.95 (9.95 to Club Members)

Book Five—1951
THE UNKINDNESS OF STRANGERS

Warner Brothers is getting it from all sides and Joe Bernardi seems to be everybody's favorite target. "A Streetcar Named Desire" is unproducible, they say. Too violent, too seedy, too sexy, too controversial and what's worse, it's being directed by that well-known pinko, Elia Kazan. To make matters worse, the country's number one hate monger, newspaper columnist Bryce Tremayne, is coming after Kazan with a vengeance and nothing Joe can do or say will stop him. A vicious expose column is set to run in every Hearst paper in the nation on the upcoming Sunday but a funny thing happens Friday night. Tremayne is found in a compromising condition behind the wheel of his car, a bullet hole between his eyes. Come Sunday and the scurrilous attack on Kazan does not

appear. Rumors fly. Kazan is suspected but he's not the only one with a motive. Consider:

Elvira Tremayne, the unloved widow. Did Tremayne slug her one time too many?

Hubbell Cox, the flunky whose homosexuality made him a target of derision.

Willie Babbitt, the muscle. He does what he's told and what he's told to do is often unpleasant.

Jenny Coughlin, Tremayne's private secretary. But how private and what was her secret agenda?

Jed Tompkins, Elvira's father, a rich Texas cattle baron who had only contempt for his son-in-law.

Boyd Larabee, the bookkeeper, hired by Tompkins to win Cox's confidence and report back anything he's learned.

Annie Petrakis, studio makeup artist. Tremayne destroyed her lover. Has she returned the favor?

$12.95 (9.95 to Club Members)

Book Six—1952
NICE GUYS FINISH DEAD

Ned Sharkey is a fugitive from mob revenge. For six years he's been successfully hiding out in the Los Angeles area while a $100, 000 contract for his demise hangs over his head. But when Warner Brothers begins filming "The Winning Team", the story of Grover Cleveland Alexander, Ned can't resist showing up at the ballpark to reunite with his old pals from the Chicago Cubs of the early 40's who have cameo roles in the film. Big mistake. When Joe Bernardi, Warner Brothers publicity guy, inadvertently sends a press release and a photo of Ned to the Chicago papers, mysterious people from the Windy City suddenly appear and a day later at break of dawn, Ned's body is found sprawled atop the pitcher's mound. It appears that someone is a hundred thousand dollars richer.

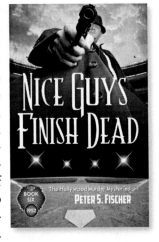

Or maybe not. Who is the 22 year old kid posing as a 50 year old former hockey star? And what about Gordo Gagliano, a mountain of a man, who is out to find Ned no matter who he has to hurt to succeed? And why did baggy pants comic Fats McCoy jump Ned and try to kill him in the pool parlor? It sure wasn't about money. Joe , riddled with guilt because the photo he sent to the newspapers may have led to Ned's death, finds himself embroiled in a dangerous game of who-dun-it that leads from L. A. 's Wrigley Field to an upscale sports bar in Altadena to the posh mansions of Pasadena and finally to the swank clubhouse of Santa Anita racetrack.

$12.95 (9.95 to Club Members)

Book Seven—1953
PRAY FOR US SINNERS

Joe finds himself in Quebec but it's no vacation. Alfred Hitchcock is shooting a suspenseful thriller called "I Confess" and Montgomery Clift is playing a priest accused of murder. A marriage made in heaven? Hardly. They have been at log-gerheads since Day One and to make mat-ters worse their feud is spilling out into the newspapers. When vivacious Jeanne d'Arcy, the director of the Quebec Film Commisssion volunteers to help calm the troubled waters, Joe thinks his troubles are over but that was before Jeanne got into a violent spat with a former lover and suddenly found herself under arrest on a charge of first degree murder. Guilty or not guilty? Half the clues say she did it, the other half say she is being brilliantly framed. But by who? Fingers point to the  crooked Gonsalvo brothers who have ties to the Buffalo mafia family and when Joe gets too close to the truth, someone tries to shut him up. . . permanently. With the Archbishop threatening to shut down the production in the wake of the scandal, Joe finds himself torn between two loyalties.

$12.95 (9.95 to Club Members)

HAS ANYBODY HERE SEEN WYCKHAM?

Everything was going smoothly on the set of "The High and the Mighty" until the cast and crew returned from lunch. With one exception. Wiley Wyckham, the bit player sitting in seat 24A on the airliner mockup, is among the missing, and without Wyckham sitting in place, director William Wellman cannot continue filming, A studio wide search is instituted. No Wyckham. A lookalike is hired that night, filming resumes the next day and still no Wyckham. Except that by this time, it's been discovered that Wyckham, a British actor, isn't really Wyckham at all but an imposter who may very well be an agent for the Russian government, The local police call in the FBI. The FBI calls in British counterintelligence. A manhunt for the missing actor ensues and Joe Bernardi, the picture's pub-

HAS ANYBODY HERE SEEN WYCKHAM?

The Hollywood Murder Mysteries
PETER S. FISCHER

licist, is right in the middle of the intrigue. Everyone's upset, especially John Wayne who is furious to learn that a possible Commie spy has been working in a picture he's producing and starring in. And then they find him . It's the dead of night on the Warner Brothers backlot and Wyckham is discovered hanging by his feet from a streetlamp, his body bloodied and tortured and very much dead. and pinned to his shirt is a piece of paper with the inscription "Sic Semper Proditor". (Thus to all traitors). Who was this man who had been posing as an obscure British actor? How did he smuggle himself into the country and what has he been up to? Has he been blackmailing an important higher-up in the film business and did the victim suddenly turn on him? Is the MI6 agent from London really who he says he is and what about the reporter from the London Daily Mail who seems to know all the right questions to ask as well all the right answers.

$12.95 (9.95 to Club Members)

Book Nine—1955
EYEWITNESS TO MURDER

Go to New York? Not on your life. It's a lousy idea for a movie. A two year old black and white television drama? It hasn't got a prayer. This is the age of CinemaScope and VistaVision and stereophonic sound and yes, even 3-D. Burt Lancaster and Harold Hecht must be out of their minds to think they can make a hit movie out of "Marty". But then Joe Bernardi gets word that the love of his life, Bunny Lesher, is in New York and in trouble and so Joe changes his mind. He flies east to talk with the movie company and also to find Bunny and dig her out of whatever jam she's in. He finds that "Marty" is doing just fine but Bunny's jam is a lot bigger than he bargained for. She's being held by the police as an eyewitness to a brutal murder of a close friend in a lower Manhattan police station. Only a

jammed pistol saved Bunny from being the killer's second victim and now she's in mortal danger because she knows what the man looks like and he's dead set on shutting her up. Permanently. Crooked lawyers, sleazy con artists and scheming businessmen cross Joe's path, determined to keep him from the truth and when the trail leads to the sports car racing circuit at Lime Rock in Connecticut, it's Joe who becomes the killer's prime target.

$12.95 (9.95 to Club Members)

ABOUT THE AUTHOR

Peter S. Fischer is a former television writer-producer who currently lives with his wife Lucille in the Monterey Bay area of Central California. He is a co-creator of "Murder, She Wrote" for which he wrote over 40 scripts. Among his other credits are a dozen "Columbo" episodes and a season helming "Ellery Queen". He has also written and produced several TV mini- series and Movies of the Week. In 1985 he was awarded an Edgar by the Mystery Writers of America. "Eyewitness to Murder" is the ninth in a series of murder mysteries set in post WWII Hollywood and featuring publicist and would-be novelist, Joe Bernardi.

TO PURCHASE COPIES OF THE HOLLYWOOD MURDER MYSTERIES. . .

Check first with your local book seller. If he is out of stock or is unable to order copies for you, go online to Amazon Books where every volume in the series is available either as a paperback or in the Kindle format.

Alternatively, you may wish to order paperback editions direct from the publisher, The Grove Point Press, P. O. Box 873, Pacific Grove, CA 93950. Each copy purchased directly will be signed by the author and personalized, if desired. If your initial order is for three or more different titles, your price per copy drops to $9.95 and you automatically become a member of the "club." Club members may purchase any or all titles in any quantity, all for the same low price of $9.95 each. In addition, all those ordering direct from the publisher will receive a FREE "Murder, She Wrote" bookmark personally autographed by the author.

TURN TO THE NEXT PAGE

for the easy-to-use order form.

Want to know more about
THE HOLLYWOOD MURDER MYSTERIES?
click on
THEGROVEPOINTPRESS. COM

ORDER FORM

To
THE GROVE POINT PRESS
P. O. Box 873
Pacific Grove, CA 93950

☐ Please send the volume(s), either one or two, checked below at $12.95 each. I understand each copy will be signed personally by the author. Also include my FREE "Murder, She Wrote" keepsake bookmark, also autographed by the author.

☐ Please send the volumes checked below (three or more) at the low price of $9.95 each. I understand this entitles me to any and all future purchases at this same low price. I also understand that each volume will be personally signed by the author. Also include my FREE "Murder, She Wrote" keepsake bookmark, also autographed by the author.

QTY

_____ *Book One—1947* **Jezebel in Blue Satin**

_____ *Book Two—1948* **We Don't Need No Stinking Badges**

_____ *Book Three—1949* **Love Has Nothing to Do With It**

_____ *Book Four—1950* **Everybody Wants An Oscar**

_____ *Book Five—1951* **The Unkindess of Strangers**

_____ *Book Six—1952* **Nice Guys Finish Dead**

_____ *Book Seven—1953* **Pray For Us Sinners**

_____ *Book Eight—1954* **Has Anybody Here Seen Wyckham?**

_____ *Book Nine—1955* **Eyewitness to Murder**

NAME _____

STREET ADDRESS _____

CITY _____

STATE _____ **ZIP** _____

Enclosed find in the amount of _____ for a total of _____ volumes. I understand there are no shipping and handling charges and that any taxes will be paid by the publisher.

ORDER FORM

To
THE GROVE POINT PRESS
P.O. Box 873
Pacific Grove, CA 93950

☐ Please send the volume(s), either one or two, checked below at $12.95 each. I understand each copy will be signed personally by the author. Also include my FREE "Murder, She Wrote" keepsake bookmark, also autographed by the author.

☐ Please send the volumes checked below (three or more) at the low price of $9.95 each. I understand this entitles me to any and all future purchases at this same low price. I also understand that each volume will be personally signed by the author. Also include my FREE "Murder, She Wrote" keepsake bookmark, also autographed by the author.

QTY

_____ *Book One—1947* **Jezebel in Blue Satin**

_____ *Book Two—1948* **We Don't Need No Stinking Badges**

_____ *Book Three—1949* **Love Has Nothing to Do With It**

_____ *Book Four—1950* **Everybody Wants An Oscar**

_____ *Book Five—1951* **The Unkindess of Strangers**

_____ *Book Six—1952* **Nice Guys Finish Dead**

_____ *Book Seven—1953* **Pray For Us Sinners**

_____ *Book Eight—1954* **Has Anybody Here Seen Wyckham?**

_____ *Book Nine—1955* **Eyewitness to Murder**

NAME _____

STREET ADDRESS _____

CITY _____

STATE _____ **ZIP** _____

Enclosed find in the amount of _____ for a total of _____ volumes. I understand there are no shipping and handling charges and that any taxes will be paid by the publisher.

ORDER FORM

To
THE GROVE POINT PRESS
P. O. Box 873
Pacific Grove, CA 93950

☐ Please send the volume(s), either one or two, checked below at $12.95 each. I understand each copy will be signed personally by the author. Also include my FREE "Murder, She Wrote" keepsake bookmark, also autographed by the author.

☐ Please send the volumes checked below (three or more) at the low price of $9.95 each. I understand this entitles me to any and all future purchases at this same low price. I also understand that each volume will be personally signed by the author. Also include my FREE "Murder, She Wrote" keepsake bookmark, also autographed by the author.

QTY

_____ *Book One—1947* **Jezebel in Blue Satin**

_____ *Book Two—1948* **We Don't Need No Stinking Badges**

_____ *Book Three—1949* **Love Has Nothing to Do With It**

_____ *Book Four—1950* **Everybody Wants An Oscar**

_____ *Book Five—1951* **The Unkindess of Strangers**

_____ *Book Six—1952* **Nice Guys Finish Dead**

_____ *Book Seven—1953* **Pray For Us Sinners**

_____ *Book Eight—1954* **Has Anybody Here Seen Wyckham?**

_____ *Book Nine—1955* **Eyewitness to Murder**

NAME _____

STREET ADDRESS _____

CITY _____

STATE _____ **ZIP** _____

Enclosed find in the amount of _____ for a total of _____ volumes. I understand there are no shipping and handling charges and that any taxes will be paid by the publisher.